TEE TIME

A FAMILY AFFAIR SPORTS NOVELLA

JEN TALTY

PRAISE FOR JEN TALTY

"*Deadly Secrets* is the best of romance and suspense in one hot read!" *NYT Bestselling Author Jennifer Probst*

"A charming setting and a steamy couple heat up the pages in an suspenseful story I couldn't put down!" *NY Times and USA today Bestselling Author Donna Grant*

"Jen Talty's books will grab your attention and pull you into a world of relatable characters, strong personalities, humor, and believable storylines. You'll laugh, you'll cry, and you'll rush to get the next book she releases!" Natalie Ann USA Today Bestselling Author

"I positively loved *In Two Weeks,* and highly recommend it. The writing is wonderful, the story is fantastic, and the characters will keep you coming back for more. I can't wait to get my hands on future installments of the NYS Troopers series." *Long and Short Reviews*

"*In Two Weeks* hooks the reader from page one. This is a fast paced story where the development of the romance grabs you emotionally and the suspense keeps you sitting on the edge of your chair. Great characters, great writing, and a believable plot that can be a warning to all of us." *Desiree Holt, USA Today Bestseller*

"*Dark Water* delivers an engaging portrait of wounded hearts as the memorable characters take you on a healing journey of love. A mysterious death brings danger and intrigue into the drama, while sultry passions brew into a believable plot that melts the reader's heart. Jen Talty pens an entertaining romance that grips the heart as the colorful and dangerous story unfolds into a chilling ending." *Night Owl Reviews*

"This is not the typical love story, nor is it the typical mystery. The characters are well rounded and interesting." *You Gotta Read Reviews*

"Murder in Paradise Bay is a fast-paced romantic thriller with plenty of twists and turns to keep you guessing until the end. You won't want to miss this one..." *USA Today bestselling author Janice Maynard*

TEE TIME

A FAMILY AFFAIR SPORTS NOVELLA

USA Today Bestseller

JEN TALTY

For my husband.

1

The sun was hours from rising, but Jack Hollister needed to see the house that his longtime friend had lived in. The house Jack lived in after his father died. The same house he'd been asked to never return to five years ago when he'd made one of the biggest mistakes of his life.

He shut down the lights, turned off the engine, and let the old rusty pickup slow to a stop down the road in the middle of nowhere South Texas. The house was set back and partially hidden behind large trees. Rudy Wade had always enjoyed his privacy along with his own private driving range and putting green in his backyard. Jack had spent much of his younger years training in that backyard.

He got out of his vehicle and leaned against the door, running his hand across his new short haircut. He was a little surprised he didn't miss his long hair or beard. He actually felt relieved to be rid of the mask he hid behind, but scared to death of who he once was, and wondered who the hell he was now. He'd lost his wife; it didn't matter that they hadn't loved each other because they nearly destroyed each other during their short marriage. He'd ruined his career. But it was losing the respect of Rudy and his daughter, Courtney, that had pushed Jack over the edge.

An image of Courtney and him playing golf flashed in his mind. She'd been his best friend, and if he were being totally honest, she was on her way to becoming a lot more until his world turned upside down.

The front porch light flickered. That was his cue to leave. He knew today would be the day, but he didn't want to see them here, at the house. No. He needed to be on common ground. A place where Jack at least felt as though he still had a leg to stand on, even if he hadn't played a serious round of golf in years.

That said, Groveland Country Club might not let him even set foot in the clubhouse, much less play a round considering his behavior the last time he'd dared set foot on the property.

He took his time, taking the back roads, letting his mind fill with memories of his youth. His father had raised him to be humble and to never take anything for granted. Somewhere from the time he'd graduated high school and the first time he'd won his first big tournament, he'd turned into an arrogant asshole and not the kind of man his father would have been proud of.

Something he needed to change.

The sun peeked out over the horizon, lightening the dark sky. Jack's pulse increased as he parked his rusty piece of shit in the back corner of the parking lot. He used to try to stand out by having the latest sports car, not by having the biggest eyesore.

The grounds crew continued to mill about as a few more cars rolled in, parking closer to the clubhouse. Every person that got out of their car glanced for an uncomfortable amount of time in Jack's direction. He couldn't blame them. An orange rusted Ford F-150 didn't fit in amongst all the Porsches, BMWs, Audis, and Land Rovers, even though it was Texas.

A white Infinity rolled to a stop in the circle in front of the bag drop, a little too close to his truck. He watched Rudy get out of his SUV. Rudy's hair had thinned a little more, and what was left had turned whiter. He'd put on a few pounds, but he still looked fit for a man pushing sixty.

Jack clutched his heart as Courtney slid out of the passenger side of the car, kissing her father's cheek. Her blond hair bounced a few inches above her shoulders. It was shorter than he'd remembered, but he liked the straight clean lines of the cut. She waved and smiled at her father as she slid into the driver's seat and turned the vehicle in his direction.

"Oh, shit!" He hit his head on the steering wheel as he ducked when she drove by. He really didn't want to be seen just yet. At least not by her. He needed to deal with Rudy first because if he said no, then it would only be Jack's pride that got crushed.

Not his heart.

He rubbed his forehead, then glanced at his watch. The pro shop didn't open until seven. He had another twenty minutes to figure out what the hell he was going to say to Rudy. He took a deep breath and pulled out a picture from the glove box.

"I miss you." He gently caressed the side of the picture. "And you." He raked his hand across his head as he stared at the two men, his father and Rudy, best friends since elementary school.

He placed the picture in his wallet and watched a few golfers pull in. He chuckled as two men looked over some new putter. The only thing Jack kept from his past was his clubs. Golfers were notorious for being a little superstitious about their equipment, and that was one of the few things that Jack absolutely held on to from that part of his life.

When he was sure the pro shop would be empty, he stepped out of his truck, squared his shoulders, and took one step at a time toward the door. He made himself take slow deep breaths as he swung the heavy wood door open. His pulse raced, and the acid in his stomach gave new meaning to painful reflux. He wanted to turn around and run when he made eye contact with Rudy, but Jack reminded himself that he was his father's son and that his father would want him to at least be man enough to come back and apologize.

"Can I help..." Rudy's pupils widened as he glanced up from whatever he was working on behind the pro shop register. "Jack?" he asked. "Is that you?"

"It's me." Jack swallowed, fighting the tears burning the corners of his eyes. "It's good to see you, Rudy."

"I can't say the same. What the hell do you want?" Rudy's eyes darkened, and he dropped his gaze to the papers in front of him.

"I'd like to talk." Jack inched forward like a scared boy about to get scolded.

"I've got nothing to say to you."

"I have some things I'd like to get off my chest, and I'd like to start with a long overdue apology."

Rudy cleared his throat, not looking up. "Okay."

"Could you at least look at me?" Jack stood on the other side of the counter, trying keep his body from trembling.

Rudy narrowed his stare and with anger flaring from his dark-brown eyes, he said, "You've apologized, now leave."

"Is this how you greeted Courtney when she came home?" Jack wanted to take the words back, along with the attitude they were laced with, the moment they left his mouth.

Rudy's chest puffed up and down like an angry bull. "Courtney's my daughter. She's always welcome in my home. You are not."

"She wasn't welcome when she ran off and married Tom when she was only eighteen, against your wishes."

Jack knew he'd just crossed the line and returned to his self-sabotaging ways. But if Rudy wasn't going to help him, then Jack might as well go back to his boat in Florida and live out his days fishing.

"That does it!" Rudy slammed his fist down on the counter. "Either you leave now, or I call the cops. Wouldn't that make a great headline? We know how much you love the negative coverage."

Jack took a deep breath. "I'm sorry, Rudy. I didn't mean that."

"Save it for someone who gives a shit."

"Well, we both know that no one does."

"And whose fault is that?" Rudy's voice softened a bit, but his expression remained hard.

"Mine," Jack said softly. "I know I hurt you."

"Hurt isn't the right word." Rudy glared at him. "What do you want?"

"I want your forgiveness," Jack said.

"Your apology is accepted. I do wish you well, but what you did, I won't soon forget, so don't expect to waltz into town and have us be friends. I don't think I can do that."

Might as well just blurt it out. "I want to golf again."

"So do it." Rudy shrugged.

"I need your help." Jack felt the blood pump unevenly through his veins as Rudy stood there, staring at him intently.

"What is it that you think I can do for you?" Rudy dropped his pencil, and he looked like he might be slightly intrigued. Or maybe amused.

Or maybe he was looking for the right moment to toss Jack out on his ass.

"I want you to be my coach again."

A golfer came into the pro shop. Abruptly, Jack turned and pretended to look at some shirts. He didn't want to be recognized until he got Rudy to agree to help him. Rudy still cared. Jack felt it, and given the right words, Rudy would help him. He had to.

A firm squeeze on the shoulder made Jack jump.

"Relax, boy," Rudy said.

Jack turned and looked into the caring eyes of the man who helped raise him. "I'm really sorry, about everything. The way I behaved on the tour. With you. How I left when I got married. I'm sorry about everything. I was wrong."

"It takes a big man to admit that," Rudy said. "I really appreciate you coming here, even after all these years to tell me that. It does mean a lot to me. But I can't teach you. You know the game, and you have the contacts. You can do it without me." Rudy dropped his hand and strolled back to the counter.

"I'm a has-been at thirty-one, and I don't want to go back with a bang. I want to do it right. Slowly, quietly, and with dignity."

That caught a hearty laugh from Rudy. "Like the way you went out?"

Jack opened his mouth to defend his actions, but there were no words to explain his drug-induced outburst.

"Sorry, son. But you certainly gave new meaning to

rebel without a cause when you tossed your driver at Tom at the Masters, practically knocking him out." A playful smile broadened Rudy's face.

"I don't care that I was higher than a kite. He deserved it," Jack muttered.

"Oh, I bet he did, considering what he did to my daughter." Silence followed for a few minutes, each man studying the other. "I can't help you," Rudy finally said, looking Jack in the eye. "I'm sorry. I'm not the coach for you."

"I guess I can understand that." Jack picked up a hat and tried it on. "I don't think I have it in me to do it alone, though. If you won't help me, there is no comeback in my future."

"That's too bad. You have some of the rawest talent I've ever seen," Rudy said. "You want to buy the hat?"

"Sure." Jack reached in his pocket and pulled out two twenties. He really shouldn't, funds were more than tight, but his pride made him do it. He took the change and headed toward the door. He gripped the handle before turning around and making a beeline for the counter. "You like to make small wagers on the golf course. Let's make a bet."

"Excuse me?"

"Play one round with me, scratch. I win, you teach. You win—"

"I won't play you."

"Come on." Jack smiled. "Whatever your handicap is trending, you can add a stroke, and that's being more than generous because I haven't played a full round since I left, unless you include miniature golf."

That caught a laugh from Rudy. "Still a no. You'd crush me. But you beat Courtney and I'll teach you. But if you lose, you walk."

Jack blinked. "Huh? You want me to play scratch golf with your daughter?"

Rudy nodded. "And, she gets three strokes." Rudy smiled like his old self, and Jack had to grip the coat rack as he thought about the last time he played Courtney.

He lost.

And he hadn't given her any strokes at all.

"You want me to do what!" Courtney Wade stared at her father with wide eyes. She wiggled her finger in her ear. She couldn't have heard him correctly.

"It's one round of golf," her father said.

"With Jack Hollister, a man we both swore if we never saw again it would be too soon. Why the hell would I play golf with him?"

"Um. I'm in the room," Jack said.

She blew out a big puff of air and continued to ignore the man she'd been trying desperately to forget for the last five years. "I'm not speaking to you, nor will I ever." She shook out her hands. "I won't do it, Dad."

"You'll do it because I asked you to," her father said with a stern tone as if she were still a teenager.

Well, she was a grown-ass adult, with a kid of her own. Just because she was living with her father while she got her life back on track didn't mean he got to tell her what to do.

"Are you crazy, Dad! Like hell I'll play him. Now if you want to smack him over the head with my driver, like he did to my ex-husband, that I might be able to do." Courtney stared Jack down, daring him to justify his actions. No matter how much he despised her ex-husband, there was no way Jack could come up with a valid reason for knocking a man unconscious.

"My days of clubbing people are over," Jack said. "And I'm surprised you're not jumping at the chance to play me again."

She tossed her head back and laughed. "Are you forgetting I beat you by two strokes?"

"Nope. I'm not." He inched a little too close for comfort. "But I was also under the influence back then. I haven't touched cocaine in a year. You'd be playing me completely drug free. Hell, I haven't even had a drink yet, but if I win, I'll buy us drinks before dinner."

"And if you do happen to beat Courtney, you will do things my way, all the way, or no deal," Rudy said.

She stood between the two men, glaring at both of them. "This is the most insane thing I've ever heard."

Her father gave her a sideways glance. The one he used to get her to do stuff all the time. "Dad. I won't play him." She waved her hand at the redhead standing so close she could feel the heat coming off his skin. The last time she'd seen Jack, he'd made her feel like she wasn't even a whole person. "He's an arrogant jerk who lies, steals, and cheats, and I don't want him around us or our golf course. This won't be good for business. The second the media catches wind of this, they will be all over us like pigs in shit. We don't need that crap. Not again. Not because of that jerk-off."

"Hello! I'm in the room," Jack said with a chuckle. He'd missed Courtney's fiery personality.

"No one cares," she said behind a clenched jaw, keeping her eyes on her father. Her insides were shaking like a volcano about to erupt.

"Nice to see you too." He leaned in front of her and smiled.

Frustrated, she pushed him aside. "Your charm doesn't work on me." Then she turned her attention back to her father. "How dare you offer a match for me. And with him." She turned to see him smiling at her. Jerk! Why the hell did he come back? She'd started to get her life back to where she wanted. The last thing she needed was a sexy, tall, muscular, red-haired wrecking ball crashing in.

"Him has a name." Jack tipped his new hat.

"You don't want to know the name we have for you," she said. "Dad, I can't believe you would even consider taking this"—if she used the word 'drunk or drug addict' she'd be a hypocrite—"thing back after everything he did to us."

"Thing?" Jack arched a brow.

"Want me to say what I'm really thinking?" She glared at him. Finally, that smug smile of his disappeared, and his eyes shifted. She'd gotten him right where it counted. Good, he deserved it.

"You should thank him for putting that ex-husband of yours in his place."

Her mouth opened, and a horrible gasp came from the pit of her stomach. "He wasn't my ex at the time," she said under her breath, rubbing her hands against her golf pants. "And he's still the father of *your* granddaughter."

"A fact we'd both like to forget," her father mumbled. "But Tom doesn't have anything to do with this."

"I just want a chance," Jack said. "I know how badly I've fucked up. I haven't two pennies to rub together, and I don't even know if I have what it takes to even make the cut."

She blinked. Not only did his voice send a warm shiver down her spine, but he looked damned good with his freshly shaved face, slender dark-blue golf slacks and white-and-blue shirt tucked neatly into his pants. "You have a lot of nerve to come waltzing in here after all these years. Do you have any idea what you did to my father?"

"I know what I did," he said. "I also know saying I'm sorry isn't enough, but it's a start. I plan on sticking around so I can show both of you just how sorry I really am."

"I've heard enough, and Courtney and I have work

to do." Her father held Jack's arm. "Tomorrow morning. Six forty-five. Game on." Her father gave her a pointed look.

"I have to take Bri to daycare." She gritted her teeth.

"I'll take her," her father said.

"What about the shop?" she questioned. "The shop opens before daycare does."

"I'll get Sandy to handle the shop while I take my granddaughter to daycare. Then I'll come and check up on you two." Her father took a step back and looked at them.

"I guess it's settled then." Jack tipped his hat toward Courtney.

"Be prepared to lose. I'm better than I was when I was a teenager," Courtney said.

"You're like a fine wine, getting better with age," Jack said, stretching out his hand.

Her father took it and shook.

She, however, turned her back. Once she heard the door close, she slumped down in one of the chairs, crossing her arms tightly across her chest. What the hell was Jack doing back in Denton? Back in her life? "How could you? You said you never wanted to see him again."

"I said the same thing to you when you told me you were pregnant, barely eighteen, and with Rivers' kid, but I didn't mean it." His comforting hand touched her shoulder. "I was angry and hurt by your actions as I was by his."

"You kicked me out," she muttered.

"You got married. You moved in with your husband." He waved to the door. "And let's not forget you only slept with Tom to piss me off, but mostly because you were so hurt by Jack getting married."

"That's not entirely true." She swallowed the bile smacking her throat. "Tom had been hitting on me for a year."

"You were seventeen, and he was in his twenties. He could have gotten arrested." Her father waggled a finger under her nose. "That's why Jack stayed away."

"No. He just wasn't interested. Tom, on the other hand, I thought he loved me."

"Don't start that again. We both know what a bastard your ex-husband is. He belongs in jail." He pulled a chair up next to her. "Have you heard from him lately?"

"He called the other day, asking about birthday stuff, but he was at his mom's so I bet it was all for show." Tom Rivers didn't love his own child. When Courtney finally got smart and left Tom, she struck a deal with him. She got full custody of Bri as long as she told the press the break-up was her doing, not his. He promised to keep her accident out of the press and she promised not to tell the world what an asshole he was. It wasn't a win-win, but it protected her daughter and that's all she cared about. "I didn't remind he's six months late on his child support and that it's been longer than that since he's seen his kid." She looked at her father as he wiped the tears from her eyes. "I called the lawyer. It's close to where we might have a case on abandonment."

"I'm with you all the way, honey. I just wish you would have fought him sooner."

She scowled. "I'm not totally innocent in all this and I'm still not sure I want to do it. He could really hurt me."

"Actually, you are innocent, but I'm not going to continue to have this same argument with you. I told you back then I'd do whatever you wanted as long as Tom stays the hell away from you and my granddaughter." He pinched the bridge of his nose. "In the meantime, I need you to lose tomorrow."

"Like hell I will." She stood, knocking a book off the desk. No way in hell would she throw a match, especially when the opponent was Jack, but more so because she didn't want him hanging around for the next few months while he trained with her father.

"I want to work with him again, and he does deserve a second chance."

"Then you should have just agreed to take him on." She tried to leave the office.

"Courtney, you always had a way with him, and I need to know what I've got to work with. The only way I know how to do that is to have him play a little competitive round with you. Please, do this for your old man."

"Damn you, Dad. I'd like nothing better than to kick his butt-ugly ass, and he'll know if I have to throw the match."

"That's a risk I'm willing to take."

"You owe me." She spun on her heels and left the office wondering why she agreed to play Jack Hollister. He was nothing but trouble. He'd come back into their lives like a whirlwind, and in the end, he'd leave a few broken hearts behind.

2

Courtney tossed her golf shoes in her locker, trying to rid the pictures of Jack from her mind, both past and present. But she couldn't shake the sense of loneliness the soft lines around his pale-green pools conveyed to the world. He'd aged a bit, and his eyes looked as if they'd seen the dark side of the universe. But his muscular frame appeared to be no worse for wear.

He had a distinctively male aroma, and he used the same damn aftershave he'd used years ago. A sexy scent that smelled like a cool breeze coming off the ocean just as the sun set over the horizon. A scent she could've lived without ever smelling again.

"How late are you going to be?" her father called as she headed out the door to pick Bri up from daycare. There had been a time she feared Tom would show up and snatch Bri right from under her nose, just to spite but he'd proven to only care about himself time and time again.

Now that Jack was back, if Tom thought Bri could be a bargaining chip of some kind, that bastard would use his own daughter to seek revenge. Courtney would have to find a way to make sure that didn't happen.

"I'm just having dinner with Nicole. I won't be late. Don't let Bri eat too much junk at the Fun Zone."

"I won't. I promise," her father said, waving as he slipped into his vehicle.

She smiled, unlocking her car door. Her father, considering everything she'd put him through, could've turned his back on her and Bri when she came crawling home, but he didn't. It warmed her heart to know that Bri was loved, regardless of who her father was.

She took a look at her watch. Just a little after five. If she was lucky, she'd make it home in time to tuck in her sweet baby girl.

She started the car and headed down the road, thinking about the way her life had turned out. Only twenty-four and she had made a mess of it, big-time.

Her father was right about one thing; she did use Tom. She wanted to get back at Jack for marrying Ms. High and Mighty Wendy Van Aken.

Courtney pulled into her favorite local watering hole and looked around for her best friend's brand-spanking-new Dodge Ram pickup. Of course, it was Texas, and there were like a dozen. Not to mention that Nicole was notorious for being late, especially now that she was a new mom. Courtney used to be annoyed by her friend's tardiness, but now she gave her a pass.

Rocki's always smelled like a sizzling hot steak, and it sent Courtney's stomach begging for food and a beer.

Shit.

Normally, she'd never drink the night before a match, but fuck it. Just one beer to take the edge off.

She followed the hostess into the back of the restaurant, ordered a beer, and sat so she could see the entrance.

With every swish of the door, she stiffened her spine, only to be disappointed. At this rate, her beer would be warm, or gone by the time Nicole showed her pretty face.

No sooner did Courtney dare to order a second beer than Nicole blew into the bar like a spinning twister. "So sorry I'm late. Besides Frankie being a moron when it comes to taking care of a baby, little Frankie doesn't like bottles, so I had to give him the boob before I left."

Courtney swallowed the guttural gasp that blasted the back of her throat. She'd had Bri shortly after her nineteenth birthday, and the beatings had already begun. She'd been careful not to drink or use drugs while she'd been pregnant, but she couldn't face her father, or Jack for that matter, after Bri had been born and she turned to the same white powder that ended Jack's career and should have ended Tom's.

God, she wished she could go back to Bri's first year

so Courtney could have been a better mother. Hell, she should have left the first time Tom hit her, but her pride got in the way.

"No worries. But I can't stay too long, and do not let me order a third, or I will be ordering a Lyft to get home."

"Oh, I wish I could have one, but not until we know little Frankie will take a bottle, and at this rate, it might be about the same time he goes off to college."

Courtney chuckled. Nicole always had a flare for the dramatic, but her laugh was cut short the second Jack strolled into the restaurant with his hands stuffed into his pants pockets. Damn slacks fit a perfectly snug around his hips, showing off his tight ass and firm legs.

Nicole glanced over her shoulder. "Is that who I think it is?"

"No," Courtney said, taking a huge swig of her beer. "It's his evil twin."

"Shit. When the hell did he get back into town?"

"He showed up at the club this morning." Courtney tried to tear her gaze away, but it was like staring at a ten-car pileup on the freeway.

He turned his head and paused midstep.

Fuck. Fuck. Fuck.

She gave him her best sarcastic smile, hoping he got the hint that she did not want to spend any more time with him.

He followed the hostess to a table on the other side of the room, thank God.

"Have you talked to him?"

"Unfortunately, my father set up a match for me against the great Jack Hollister tomorrow," Courtney said, leaning forward. "But don't you dare say a word to anyone. I don't want people showing up at the club, especially the media. I couldn't handle being in the spotlight again, especially since things have finally died down from the divorce and my custody battle." She'd spent three hellish years married to Tom, but that wasn't half as bad as the horrors he put her through when she finally wised up and left.

Tom Rivers was the golden child of the PGA. No one dared speak badly of him. Well, not to his face, or in public because Tom had connections, and he'd find your weak spot, then exploit it until he could ruin you.

"My lips are sealed, but what about Wendy and her father? Don't they still live around here?"

"Don't remind me." Courtney swallowed the vomit that trickled up her esophagus. "Wendy was in the club the other day, and she felt the need to remind me that my father doesn't have a winner in his back pocket. Hell, he hasn't coached anyone since Jack left."

"Wendy and her dad destroyed that," Nicole said.

From the moment Jack moved into Courtney's family home when his father had passed away, Wendy had made it known that she planned on having Jack for her own. She constantly gave Courtney a hard time and treated her like shit. Wendy tossed her beauty and money around and flaunted her bedroom eyes everywhere, and she enjoyed letting Courtney know the moment she got Jack in bed. As a matter of fact, she walked out of the bedroom, tucking her stockings into her purse, and smiled at Courtney as if she'd just won the lottery.

"Yeah, but Jack let them." Courtney and her father could blame Wendy and her dad until they were blue in the face, but Jack was the one that fired Rudy in the first place, and that hurt.

"He was young and green."

"He was arrogant and let money and fame taint why he played the game in the first place." When Courtney had first realized she'd fallen head over heels in love with Jack, she had been just short of eighteen and about to graduate from high school. She had been spending a lot of time with Jack, helping him get ready to try to make a sweep of the majors. He'd been favored to be on the top of the money list, and her father worked with him almost every day.

Courtney had trained with Jack as much as possible. At first, her father didn't like them being together so much. He thought they had too much fun on the course instead of concentrating on the fundamentals. But when Jack got his first big win and she got her full ride to college on a golf scholarship, her father let it go. She and Jack were good for each other. Both highly competitive, and while he was a much better golfer, that only pushed her and by the time she came to the end of her high school career, she a minus one.

She had her own plans to go pro.

But that all went up in a bundle of smoke the day Bri was born. Not that she ever regretted having her baby girl, but she did regret the decisions she made that led up to the birth of her daughter.

And she never did play college golf, nor a single professional round. She'd come to terms with both.

But sitting in the restaurant, staring at Jack's back, she knew she'd never really dealt with her feelings for Jack, and she probably never would.

"He made a mistake. We all do."

"I realize that," Courtney said. "I mean, Wendy and her father offered him the world. But he had to leave my father's supervision, and he couldn't train with me anymore; otherwise, James Van Aken would take his money and his daughter elsewhere." Courtney thought for sure Jack had started to notice her that year. Their age difference seemed to become immaterial, and once she turned eighteen, it wouldn't matter anymore. They had a deep connection, or at least she thought so. Then she had the brilliant idea to tell him how she felt. That didn't go too well. A few weeks later, Jack married Wendy in a tacky chapel in Vegas. Courtney slept with Tom and ended up pregnant, and subsequently miserable and in an abusive marriage.

Bri was the only good thing in her life, besides her father.

"So, what is this match all about? And are you going to play him?" Nicole asked just as her phone buzzed. She glanced at the screen. "Crap. It's Big Frankie. I better take it."

"Go ahead."

When Courtney gave birth to Bri, Tom had been in

some hotel snorting coke with some groupie getting his rocks off. She told herself then that she'd get her act together, but it took another year and a half before that happened.

"I'm sorry, I've got to go," Nicole said. "Big Frankie's mom went bonkers at the nursing home, and he's got to go deal with that."

If Courtney didn't know the situation better, she'd wonder if her friend was trying to ditch her for greener pastures. "Code red bonkers?"

"Big Frankie said she stabbed someone with a butter knife thinking they were trying to poison her. She's becoming more and more violent, and we just don't know what to do." Nicole swiped at her eyes. "She doesn't even know who we are anymore. Not even a glimmer of recognition. It's killing Frankie, and that's just eating away at my heart so bad that I actually suggested we move her in with us."

"You both know with a new baby that's probably not possible." Courtney reached across the table and took her friend's hand. "Go. Next week, we'll just bring the kids with us."

"Sounds like a plan." Nicole smiled. "Now, do yourself a favor. Go over and talk to him because I know you want to."

"Nope." Courtney shook her head. "I'm getting my dinner to go, and then I'm out the door." And she meant it. No way would she commiserate with the enemy.

"I'll call you tomorrow." Nicole raced out of the

restaurant, stopping at the door to wave frantically before she disappeared into the warm Texas night air.

Courtney fiddled with the label on her beer bottle while she waited for the waitress to bring her dinner. She opted to eat alone at the bar versus alone at home. Her father and Bri wouldn't be back for another hour, so she might as well eat her burger while it's hot.

"What happened to Nicole?" Jack asked as he made himself comfortable.

"She had to go home," Courtney admitted.

"That's too bad." He flashed her a sexy grin. "Why don't you have dinner with me?"

She laughed. "Why the hell would I do that?"

"So, we can talk and maybe clear the air."

"Look," she said, letting out a long breath. "I'm going to do what my father asked and play you tomorrow. But then it's adios, my friend."

"Friend, I like that." He tipped his beer.

"We're not friends anymore. You killed that when you married Wendy, fired my father, and walked out on both of us."

"Jealousy was never very becoming on you."

"I wasn't jealous, Jack. I was concerned. And I was right." She lifted her glass with a faint knowing smile.

"So was I." He lifted his brow.

Her smile faded. "Just leave." She choked on the lump that settled in the back of her throat when he took her hand.

"I'm sorry I hurt you." He tilted his head, catching her gaze. "I was young and arrogant, and I wanted it all right then and there, and I didn't care who I stepped on to get it."

"What's different now?" She pulled her hand from his.

"I suppose I deserved that."

If she really wanted to be mean, she could remind him of his violent outburst on the golf course the day before his career ended, but discussing his temper might bring up Tom's, and no way would she ever admit to Jack that Tom ever left a mark on her body.

"It wasn't a dig," she said. "It was an actual honest question. I don't know what you've been doing for the last four years. I haven't a clue as to where you've been. You literally disappeared. There wasn't even a sighting of you anywhere since you appeared in court after..." She let the thought dangle in the air. They both knew what she was referring to.

A long silence filled the space while the waitress brought their food.

"I guess not much has changed if you were arrogant enough to think I'd eat with you." She dunked her fry into the ketchup and plopped it into her mouth.

"Not true. I told the waitress to bring it over but to be prepared for me to be kicked to the curb, and since I already gave up my table, it meant either eating at the bar or taking it to my pickup." He leaned back and lifted his arms, holding his palms to the ceiling. "So, can I stay? I'm buying."

Don't do it. Don't do it. Don't do it. "Well, if you're footing the bill, why not?" She shrugged. She'd rather eat a hot meal with bad company than a cold one alone.

Asshole had the nerve to smile. "You look good."

"You look like the same cocky asshole that broke my father's heart."

That wiped the smug grin off his face. "I'm not," he said, dropping his burger to his plate. "I spent three years basically trying to drink or drug myself to death and let me tell you, I came close a couple of times." He tapped at his chest. "About a year ago, I had a come to Jesus moment."

"I don't mean to be rude, but I don't care."

He laughed. "I can tell."

"For the record, I'm only doing this because my father asked me to." She shoved her empty beer bottle to the side. "And because I will enjoy kicking your ass."

"Rudy said I had to give you three strokes, but honestly, you won't need it. If I was a smart man, and we both know I'm not the brightest bulb in the closet, I'd be a no-show tomorrow."

"If you decide not to come, let me know. That will give me a little more time with my daughter in the morning," Courtney said.

"How is Bri?" Jack tossed his napkin on the plate and leaned back, folding his arms. When he'd walked out of her life for good, Bri had been about a year old and while Jack hadn't spent much time with Bri, the few times he'd seen her, he'd been great with her. "She's almost five, right?"

No mother would ever forget the day their child

was born, but Bri's birth hadn't been the miraculous event that most parents bragged about. It had been a night from hell that Jack had a front row seat for. Thankfully, she didn't think Jack knew about the abuse because her father hadn't figured it out until after Bri had been born.

Courtney nodded. The memories of Bri's first night on this earth flooded her mind. It was both one of the worst and best days of her life. "She's amazing."

"She has you as a mom; of course she is."

"Don't say that," Courtney snapped. "You don't know me. You haven't known me in years, if you ever really knew me, so stop acting like we're old friends." She gathered up her belongings. "Whatever you do, don't you dare go breaking my father's heart because this Courtney." She pointed to herself as she stood. "You don't want to fuck with."

3

The following morning Courtney awoke with a slight headache and the worst case of nerves she ever had. With the sun barely peeking over the horizon, Courtney dropped the bucket of balls and started warming up.

One thing she loved about living with her father was that she could start her day doing the one thing she loved almost as much as her daughter, swinging a golf club. Playing the game competitively had lost its allure when she married Tom. Her life soured completely the moment she slept with Tom in the name of revenge. The only thing that kept her going was Brianna.

She glanced over her shoulder and smiled while Bri practiced her chipping. She'd made it clear she wasn't going to be a golfer, and both Courtney and her father were fine with that announcement.

Courtney lined up the ball and swung.

Splat!

"Crap." She sliced the ball into the water hazard her father built to the right of the putting green.

"Mind elsewhere?" her father teased.

Focusing on the flag, she ignored her father and landed her next shot about six inches from the cup.

"Stay mad at me and you'll crush him," her father said.

"Crush who?" She switched clubs, and flags, going for some distance. "Damn it!" She watched as her out-of-control backswing created a slice, landing her ball about ninety yards right and forty yards short.

"Too much—"

"The last thing I need right now is you in my head." She dropped another ball on the grass and took a practice swing, stopping at the top to remind her of where her backswing should be. Checking the flag one last time, she addressed the ball and…

Whack!

"Nice swing, honey. Relax, either way I'm gonna take him back. He needs me." Her dad stood closer, getting another ball ready for her, holding her club in the air. "Rotate faster." He nudged her hip.

She swung, smacking the ball on the sweet spot, and inwardly smiled. "I think you need him." She didn't glance up, just addressed the ball her father placed and concentrated on avoiding the dreaded slice. Her downfall.

"I miss him," her father admitted.

"I know you do." She looked at her dad, who looked

out over the driving range. "I won't lose on purpose. I have too much pride to do that, but we both know, Jack, even on a bad day, will most likely beat me."

He chuckled. "Never thought you would toss the game, and we both know you have what it takes to be the best. Hit your driver, then we'll go. You can practice your putting at the course."

She rolled her eyes. "Sure thing, boss." She pulled her driver out as her father stood back, hands on hips, analyzing her swing. Starting at about the age of five, she had to learn to deal with the great Rudy scrutinizing every aspect of her game. For the most part, it didn't bother her, but right now, he was getting under her skin.

After hitting a great drive, she collected her things and followed her father and daughter back to the house.

The ride to the course was anything but quiet. Bri had heard them talking about Jack. She didn't remember him, but she knew who he was, and she wanted to come meet him. Courtney wasn't sure she ever wanted Jack and Bri to meet, but if he was here for more than a few more days, it would happen, and then Bri would tell Tom, and that wouldn't be good.

"Have a good day, baby." Courtney kissed Bri's cheek, giving her a big hug. "I love you."

"Mommy? Will I see my daddy on my birthday?"

Courtney's heart stopped. She'd tried so hard not to make Tom look like a monster in her baby's eyes. An almost five-year-old didn't need to know that her father had not only demoralized and beat her mother, but almost raped her as well. "Oh, sweetie, if he can't make it, Grandpa will make up for Daddy not being there. And Chuck E. Cheese can't wait to meet you; he told me so." She batted Bri's nose, hoping she once again distracted her enough. She asked so few questions about her father that Courtney hoped she'd eventually forget him.

"Play good, Mommy," Bri said. "I hope you kick Jack's butt."

"Me too."

"I'll come check on you as soon as I get back," her father said from behind the steering wheel.

"Thanks, Dad." Courtney stood in the parking lot and watched her car disappear between the trees. There were days she didn't think she deserved such a wonderful little girl. She just hoped she wasn't screwing Bri up too badly.

Once on the putting green, Courtney concentrated on the short game. Her putting had always been the strongest part of her game; it's how she managed to beat Jack the last time she played him stroke for stroke. What she lacked in distance, she made up for in her ability to one-putt most of the time. And those one-putts came from her ability to place the ball near the pin when she chipped.

Jack tended to get greedy on the course, and he made aggressive second shots, often getting himself in trouble. She'd take a nice par any day of the week than ending up with a bogey because she missed an up-and-down opportunity.

"Nice stroke," Jack said softly as if not to startle her.

But her insides jumped anyway. "Thanks," she muttered, not looking up, but setting up another putt. For the last few years, she'd hoped she could just forget about the 'jolly green giant.' She laughed out loud. It had been a long time since she'd remembered Jack in terms of the nickname she'd come up with for him years ago.

"What?"

"Trust me, you don't want to know."

"Okay." He lined up a putt and missed.

She lined up the same putt, and...

Clank.

The ball bounced successfully in the cup. She smiled and tipped her visor to him. God, she'd missed him.

Way too much.

"I'm sunk if you keep putting like that."

"Maybe you need to worry about your own game." Butterflies floated around in her stomach. He could still get to her.

"Let's get the show on the road." He yanked his clubs and pulled the bag on his back. They clanked with each step he took toward the first tee.

"Same rules as always?" She set her bag down near the men's tees. She planned on playing from them, but he needed to play from the professional tees.

He shrugged as he took one last stretch and then

placed his ball on a tee. He took a practice swing, then glanced over his shoulder. "A three, huh?"

"Nope. I'm actually a one, but you always gave me three strokes, and I'm gonna keep them. How've you been playing?" She worried some about her ability to beat him. His game was always at his best when he was a little rusty.

He turned and waggled the club, did his little dance with his feet before his body stilled for a second, and then he swung, perfectly.

"Nice." She followed the ball's slight fade as it landed dead center about three hundred and twenty yards down the fairway on a short par four. "Damn."

"Last time I played a full round that I kept score, I hit two over, but that was a while ago. For the last month, I've just been practicing."

"You never liked to just hit balls."

"I told you. I've changed."

They walked to the men's tee box where she had about ten yards, but her drives, even if they went straight, couldn't match his. This time she came close, about two hundred and ninety-five yards. She smiled. Her first tee shot usually set the tone. It was going to be a good round.

By the ninth hole they were even, both at one under, which meant Courtney was winning. His frustration didn't go unnoticed. While he hit the ball well, he couldn't putt to save his life. "Do you want a drink?" she asked him as they made the turn.

"Gatorade would be nice." He took his putter out

and made a few short strokes in the grass while he waited.

Courtney couldn't help but notice how uncomfortable Jack looked. She didn't know if it was her or the game. Whenever they'd play in the past, he'd been easy-going, relaxed, and carefree. Today he seemed to be wound tighter than a forty-year-old virgin.

"If you don't mind me saying, you're pushing all your putts," she said after he missed an easy five-footer for birdie.

"Really? Ya don't say." He addressed the ball and hit the crap out of it. Getting angry had always been good for his long game, but not so good for his putting.

"Well, then use it." She huffed as they headed down the fairway. "Just—"

"Okay, Rudy." He glared at her.

"Just trying to help," she said bitterly. Why she wanted to help him was beyond her. He broke her heart and would do it again if she gave him half a chance.

"You don't want me around. So why the pointer?" He studied his putt, addressed the ball, and sent it toward the cup.

"I see you still can take direction," she teased when the ball landed in the cup with a clank. She looked up at him and vertigo set in. She held her hands out to the sides and tried to stable herself. If only she'd taken her putter with her.

"Court?" He held her by the biceps.

"I'm fine." She shrugged him off and headed for the next tee.

He hit his ball and then gave her a displeasing look. It wasn't as bad as the day she'd told him that she was pregnant and getting married. No, that day he looked like he bit into a lemon. This was more of a look as if the sun were in his eyes, making him squint.

"What?" she asked.

"What made you dizzy?"

"Out in the sun," she said, stepping in front of the ball. She knew the second she started the swing she should have stopped. She mumbled a few choice profanities over his chuckles as her ball went sailing to the right rough.

For the next few holes they remained quiet. He'd gotten two birdies, and this last hole he chipped in for eagle. This put him at five under, with her at even. He was in the lead, with only one hole to go. He'd have to really screw up and she'd have to do the impossible to catch him.

"I concede." She sighed. Match over. She'd lost. And not because she couldn't beat him, but because she let him get into her head. A mistake she swore she'd never let happen again.

"Care to up the stakes? Do or die on the last hole?" His smooth voice rippled across the tee box, landing in her ears and sending a warm shiver down her spine.

Now she just had to keep him out of her heart.

She squared her shoulders, looking at him head-on. "Will you go away if I beat you?"

"No," he said flatly. "I want to golf again. I need this, Courtney. I need your dad."

His level stare left her feeling unstable. Spots danced in front of her eyes, and she swayed. Feeling like she would fall over, she sat down on the bench. The motion sickness had been getting better. She only seemed to be having issues when she was in elevators, planes, occasionally glancing up at the sky, or anything she wasn't in control of. She wasn't in control of anything at present. "If you won't go away, then there's nothing left to bet."

"Why?" He took a step closer to her.

"Why!" Abruptly, she stood and fell over when a sudden wave of nausea attacked her senses.

He knelt at her side in seconds. "What the?" He took her hand and helped her up. "Are you sick?"

"I told you, I'm fine. I just had a dizzy spell from standing up too quickly and from being in the sun all morning." She pushed him away, looking down at the ground.

He cupped her chin. His fingers glided across her face. His green eyes filled with compassion as he tilted her head. "You almost passed out. What's going on?"

"If you must know, I suffer from vertigo. I had a concussion a while back, and for some strange reason, every once in a while, I feel like I'm on a roller coaster. But it's getting better." She batted his hand away. The unwanted sensations his touch gave to her made her vertigo seem miniscule. No mistaking he still had the same effect he always had on her, and she resented the hell out of him for it.

"How'd you get a concussion?" he asked as if he cared.

"None of your damned business." She managed to calm herself and walked, though a bit shakily, to her clubs. "Since you won, I'd like to call it a match."

"I'd like to finish the last hole." He stepped in front of her.

"Be my guest." Taking the time to play another hole with him, looking at him, wishing he had returned her feelings all those years ago, she didn't need to torture herself anymore. She'd done what her father asked, and if her father chose to get back into the coaching game, then so be it. She would just have to ask both of them to leave her out of it. She'd forgive Jack, but she wouldn't become his friend. Not again. Her heart couldn't take it.

"With you. I've really missed you." He pulled her clubs off her shoulders.

She froze, unable to move or speak. She sucked in as much oxygen as she could, but she couldn't release it from her lungs. She just stood there and stared at him, screaming at herself to run and run fast.

His strong hands lifted her visor off her head and smoothed away a few stray hairs that had fallen from her ponytail. "I'm so sorry, Courtney," he whispered, cupping her face. "You have no idea how sorry I am. I've thought about you every day."

She looked into his green Irish eyes and melted. Her heart pounded as the blood in her veins pumped with unsteady bursts throughout her body. She opened her mouth, but only a grunt escaped her lips. Five years ago, she gave him the opportunity to love her, and he looked at her with disgust in his eyes. Today, those same green pools looked at her as if she were the center of the universe, but that wasn't possible. Jack thought only of himself. She was just a pawn in his plan to get back in the circuit.

"I wish I understood then, what I understand now." He traced her cheekbones with his thumbs. "I wish I thought it would be okay to feel the way I did."

"What are you talking about?" she managed to squeak out.

He tilted his head and moved even closer. So close she thought he might kiss her. *Oh, God. He wouldn't dare.*

She blinked.

Then his soft lips brushed hers, sending shockwaves from her head to her toes.

"Courtney," he whispered, pulling her against him.

He felt strong, and she felt like she had just come home from a long and exhausting journey. Lifting up on tiptoe, she wrapped her arms around his broad shoulders and gave in to his kiss. It was too sweet not to. Too tender not to be real, and damn it, too good to pass up. She'd dreamed about what it would be like to be kissed, really kissed, by Jack Hollister since she'd been sixteen years old. She knew back then it was a pipe dream, but she figured when she became an adult, everything would change.

Boy, had she gotten that wrong.

He pressed his hands on her back, pressing his body hard against hers. His tongue, warm and tasting of peppermint, danced inside her mouth, sending shock waves to the soft spikes on her golf shoes. She lost herself in the moment, the dream, until the sound of a golf cart pulled her back to reality.

"Damn you." She pushed him away, trying desperately to slow her breathing. "How could you?" she muttered, turning from him.

"What? All I did was kiss you."

"Why? Why did you do that? Because I remember a time, a few years ago, when I kissed you and was told to go home to daddy."

"That was different."

"Oh. You're right. I was a stupid, starry-eyed kid who didn't know any better. I had a crush on a washed-up drug addict, and I didn't marry much better."

He turned from her and grabbed his driver. "Finish the damned hole." He addressed the ball and let it rip, straight down the fairway.

Jack stood under the cold water in the locker room trying to cool his emotions. But it didn't help. The kiss had come out of nowhere, but, God, it felt right. And Courtney was more beautiful than he remembered. He felt the same way about her as he did the last time he saw her.

Confused. Conflicted.

And totally infatuated.

When Courtney came to him five years ago, declaring her love, he almost choked on his beer. He had been halfway to drunk when she had shown up. And her confession only made him want to drown in a vat of beer even more. He'd been having feelings for Courtney since before it would be considered appropriate. He used Wendy to try to change that, but it backfired. If Wendy hadn't just told him she was pregnant just hours before, he might not have pushed Courtney away that night.

But none of that mattered now.

Once he changed into a fresh set of clothes, he headed for the grillroom since Rudy wanted to talk. Lay out the plan for Jack's quiet comeback, so to speak. This was what he wanted, so why was he so damned scared?

Rudy sat at a corner table with Courtney. They looked deep in discussion. Jack really didn't want to go over and interrupt them, but then Courtney bolted from her chair and took off. She uttered a few profanities as she flew by him.

"Sit." Rudy offered him a chair, rubbing his jaw. "What do you want?"

"To play again," Jack answered.

Rudy shifted in his chair. "To play? Be on top? Or to come home?" He looked Jack in the eye.

"The golf course is home." Jack's palms broke out in a cold sweat.

"I don't work the same way as Van Aken."

"I'm not looking for a promoter, a sponsor, or anything like what I was before." The only thing Van Aken offered Jack, besides an ulcer, had been money and coverage, but neither one had been worth it. "I want a teacher and mentor. I want to ease myself back in. Play in all the smaller tournaments. Start from the bottom and work my way up. I want what you and I started all those years ago."

"And can you agree to stay out of the limelight?" Rudy questioned him as if he could read his thoughts.

"Hell yes."

"If we do this, it's my way or hit the road, Jack." Rudy's gaze never wavered. "Are we in agreement?"

"What exactly do you want me to do?" Jack had worked with Rudy for years. He had some pretty unconventional ways of doing things. One newspaper deemed him the 'outlaw golf doctor.' Jack could deal with whatever Rudy tossed in his direction, as long as it meant Rudy was his teacher and not someone else.

"Whatever I tell you, starting with moving into the house."

"Nah-uh. No way." Jack shook his head vigorously.

"Then no deal." Rudy leaned back in his chair and crossed his arms. He had this look that told Jack this could be a dealbreaker.

"What does Courtney say?" Just the sound of her name, rolling off his tongue reminded him of how good she felt against his body, her lips on his skin, and the passion in her embrace. Today wasn't the first time he had felt it.

"She threatened to move out. Doesn't think it's good for you to be around Bri." Rudy leaned closer. "How much money do you have?"

"I'm surviving."

"How bad?" Rudy put a sturdy hand on his shoulder.

"Bad enough," Jack admitted. "I can't pay you."

"Having you back will be payment enough. No drugs, no staying out late, and no girls."

"I can live with that, but I can't live in your house."

"You don't have a choice. I need to know where you are and what you're doing." Rudy stood, waving his hand toward the door.

Jack followed. "I don't blame you for not trusting me. I wouldn't in your shoes. But, and I mean no disrespect, Courtney doesn't want me there, and I think we should consider her thoughts and feelings in all this."

"I have." Rudy walked to Jack's pickup where Courtney had perched herself, not looking so happy. "Give me your keys." Rudy held his hand out.

Jack pulled his keys out, handing them to Rudy, thinking he should hightail it back to Galveston and go back to being a nothing. "Why?"

"Courtney will drive you to collect your belongings."

The acid in Jack's stomach hit the back of his throat. He clutched the center of his chest. He grimaced as he choked the bile down and looked in the cab of his pickup for the Tums. He popped two, feeling four eyes piercing into his back.

"We still have a deal?" Rudy looked between Courtney and him.

"Not if she's gonna leave on my account."

"She has nowhere else to go."

"I could go back to Tom," she said.

Rudy narrowed his gaze. "Don't you dare ever joke about that, young lady."

Jack stepped back, feeling the rage coming from Rudy's rigid body. He glanced at Courtney. Her eyes welled with tears. He'd known her marriage to Tom hadn't been good, but he got the distinct impression bad only scratched the surface.

"This wasn't such a good idea. I didn't come here to cause problems with the two of you, though I am glad I got to apologize. Now, give me my keys, and I'll just go back to where I came from."

Courtney sighed. "Get in the damned car, Jack." She climbed behind the steering wheel of her small SUV and started the engine.

He looked to Rudy for advisement. Rudy nodded, so Jack got in the car.

"Where are we off to?" she asked, pulling out of the parking lot.

"Traveler's Motel, outside of town." His hands smacked the dashboard as the SUV lunged to the right. "You heard correctly," he muttered, shame gripping his heart.

"That place is a dump." Courtney's voice seemed softer.

"No kidding. I'm sorry about all of this."

She laughed. "No, you're not. Just the same old selfish Jack. Thinking only of yourself and no one else." The anger in her words matched the jolting of her vehicle.

"That's bull." He turned to look at her. "I never expected him to make me move in."

"Save it. You moved in the last time you started training."

"I was fifteen and had no place to go. Christ, Courtney. My father had just died. What would you have me do?" Jack got out of the SUV before she even put it in park. "I'll only be a few minutes." He slammed the door shut, turned his back, and headed for his room.

"Ouch!" She stopped the hotel door from hitting her in the face.

"I don't need your help." He tried to push her outside, but she had already entered the pathetic room that smelled of stale eggs left out on a hot summer day.

He had his one and only other golf shirt hanging to dry, along with his other pants. "I lost it all. Satisfied?" He stuffed everything he owned in his duffel bag. "I just have to settle the bill." He stormed off, leaving her standing in his simple but pathetic existence.

4

Courtney listened to her father tell Bri the story of the *Three Billy Goats Gruff*. Courtney couldn't help but feel all warm and fuzzy as her father deepened his voice and Bri giggled in delight. Just like Courtney had when she had been a small child.

"Grandpa?" Bri sighed.

Courtney stepped closer to the half-open door to listen.

"Jack's sad," Bri said.

"I think you might be right, but I'm sure you can cheer him up."

"How?"

Courtney didn't listen to the rest. She didn't want to know her father's plans for her daughter to make Jack feel better because then she might taint them, and that would be a horrible thing to do to a child.

Besides, Courtney understood Jack's pain, the lost, lonely feeling of starting over. Facing your deepest, darkest demons head-on, unable to stop the thundering crash of all your hopes and dreams of the past, only to have to rebuild them all.

Remembering the look of utter despair plastered on Jack's face back at the two-bit hotel made Courtney want to scream. He had to know they'd already figured out he was broke. Hell, no shame in that. But if Jack had the money, he probably wouldn't have come running back to her father in the first place.

"Damn him," she muttered just as her father came out of Bri's bedroom.

"Me?" He looked playfully at her.

"No, Jack. He's just using us."

"I don't think so." Her father squeezed her shoulder. "But if it will make you feel better to think the worst of him, go ahead. But don't forget how people treated you, especially not knowing the entire story about what happened between you and Tom." Her father arched a brow. "We really don't know what's happened to him in the last couple of years, but it can't be good."

"Damn you now." She glared at her father, knowing he was right. She was just looking for a way to hate Jack, because her true feelings were unmentionable. And impossible. Courtney slipped into Bri's room. "Hey there, sweetheart."

"Mommy?" Bri looked up at Courtney from under the covers.

"What baby?" Courtney sat down on the bed, brushing Bri's bouncy blond curls from her face. She had her father's hair, but she looked like Courtney and smelled like bubbles.

"You like Jack? I like Jack." Bri smiled wide.

Boy, did Bri like Jack. She had sat on his lap, pulled him all over the house, and even had him laughing.

"He's okay." Courtney curled up next to her daughter, snuggling in close. "I've known him a long time."

"Daddy hates him."

"When did you talk with your dad about Jack?" Courtney sat up in alarm. If Tom had spoken to Bri, he'd be breaking their agreement. He was supposed to go through her first, but it wouldn't be the first Tom did things his own way.

"Today," Bri said innocently.

"Daddy called?" Courtney's stomach twisted.

"Yep."

"When? Did Grandpa talk to him?" Courtney tried not to upset her daughter.

"Grandpa wasn't happy about it."

"Did you have a nice talk with Daddy?"

"We talked about the party." Bri shrugged her shoulders. "He's not coming," she said, like it didn't matter. "Can Jack come?" Her eyes glistened in the reflection of the nightlight.

"Sure." The single word flew from her mouth with excitement. "I mean, if you want and he doesn't have plans." She shouldn't be happy her daughter wanted Jack to come to her party. She should be concerned about her little girl getting too attached to the all-too-charming Jack Hollister.

Bri giggled. "He lives here now, Mommy. How could he have other plans? Gosh, you're so silly." Bri gave Courtney a big kiss. "Night, Mommy."

"Night, baby." Courtney slipped out of her daughter's room. She rubbed her temples and headed down to the kitchen where her father sat at the table, reading the latest *Golf Digest*.

"Jack said you had some dizzy spells on the course." He glanced over the magazine.

"The doctor said they could still happen," she said.

"He said you fell over."

"I was in the hot sun all day and under pressure. I stood up too quickly." She reached out and touched her father's face. "I have a doctor's appointment next week. I will talk with him about it then."

"I don't want anything to happen to you." He kissed her hand. "I love you."

"I love you too, Dad," she said. "Were you going to tell me about Tom's call today?"

Her father glanced over his shoulder toward the stairway. "Tom heard through the grapevine that Jack was at the club today. He couldn't get ahold of me there, so he called the house. She got to the phone before I could answer it, and the asshole asked her about Jack."

"What did she tell him?" Courtney held her breath.

"The truth. We can't ask a five-year-old to lie."

"That's true." Courtney took a bottle of wine from the beverage cooler and filled a portable tumbler. "So, Tom knows Jack is living with us.

That's going to cause problems. How long did he talk to Bri?"

"Only a couple of minutes. When I asked for the phone, she handed it over pretty quickly, but Tom was defiantly strung out on something, and he all but threatened to come after you."

"If I wasn't afraid he could beat me in a custody case, I'd tell him to bring it." If only she'd come to her father the first time Tom had hit her.

If only she never started doing cocaine.

Or taking pills.

If only she'd been a stronger person all those years ago.

"I wish you would ask him to give up his parental rights all together, or fight him on it," her father said. They'd had this argument more than once, and she was glad her father opted to shut it down before it got heated. "Listen, Jack is out back practicing. He's doing everything I'm asking; now I need you to help me."

"You want me to go analyze his swing, watch his short game, and give you my opinion in the morning."

"You're an amazing teacher," her father said. "You have a real talent for the game, but you have an ability to fix people's swings."

"I learned that from you, Dad." She tipped her wine glass and took a sip. "I'll go see what's he's doing." She snagged the bottle. "I hate to admit it, but he's still got it." She tucked the bottle into a portable cooler along with another tumbler, assuming Jack might like a glass or two. "If he's truly changed, he's got a real shot."

"You don't believe he's a different man?"

"I haven't spent enough time with him, but I know from experience we all can change."

Her father leaned in and kissed her cheek. "I don't believe that is true of your ex-husband."

"I know you don't like to hear this, but if he could ever stop doing drugs and give up chasing tail, he's not the horrible person you think he is."

Her father drew his lips into a tight line. "After what he did to you, I can't believe you'd even think that."

"I'm not saying I forgive him, or that I want him near my daughter, but he does have some redeeming qualities." She patted her father's chest. "As does Jack." Comparing Tom to Jack was like comparing a Kia Soul to a Range Rover Sport, but her father got the point. "Knowing Jack, he'll either be sitting on the big rock pretending to practice, or he'll actually do what you want, and he'll be at it until I make him call it quits. Either way, don't wait up." She didn't wait for her father to respond. She made a beeline for the back door and the driving range.

The large lights lit up the backyard, dimming the moon and the stars. The sound of metal hitting a ball echoed in the cool night. Quietly, she made herself comfortable on the bench and watched Jack take swing after swing.

"I can't get rid of this slight hook," he said, teeing up another ball and lining up his driver. "I'm so used to correcting for a slice that I'm not sure what to do."

"For now, keep swinging."

"I can't even feel what I'm doing wrong, and that's making me nuts."

"Give me five more swings, and I'll tell you." She crossed her legs and soaked in his muscular frame.

He raised the club and swung. "Are you my coach now?"

"I work with my father, and he sent me out here to observe. I'll report to him what I see, and he won't mind if I tell you in the process." Her body trembled; her blood pumped unevenly through her veins, and her breathing became slightly erratic.

"You always knew my game better than anyone." He set his club in the caddy and meandered toward her, taking the glass of wine she offered. "So, why am I hooking the ball?"

"You're lifting your left hip before you even start your swing. It's subtle, but you're doing it, making you draw the ball to the left."

"Impressive."

"You're an asshole." She scooted to the other side of the bench, making sure there was a safe distance between them. "You did that on purpose."

"No. Actually, I didn't, but now that you say it, I can feel that's what I was doing, which means I'm probably leaning into my swing when chipping from a hundred and twenty yards out." He stretched out his legs and crossed his ankles.

She focused her gaze on the silhouette of his plump lips as he raised the tumbler to his mouth. "I won't be doing a lot of this in the coming weeks."

"Training is about to get real intense."

"Which is why I want to make sure we put the past behind us."

"I'm doing exactly that," she said, losing the ability to fight. It was too hard to be angry all the time.

"I never meant to hurt you." He rested a hand on her thigh. "I'm so sorry. If I could go back..."

She brushed his hand away and stood. "There's no going back. Only moving forward."

"I made a lot of mistakes. Especially with you."

Her breath hitched. Looking into his warm green eyes, she saw the man she once knew. "We were both young, and honestly, I don't want to dwell on it anymore."

"Neither do I," he said. "Especially since we'll be training together again."

"That won't be happening." Sure, she'd help her father now and again by analyzing Jack's swing, or watching a hole or two, but she wouldn't become his caddy or his training partner again. No way. She had a job at the pro shop and her own lessons to give. This was her father's gig, and Jack was in good hands.

"I can't do this without you."

"Yes. You can." She leaned over and kissed his cheek. "When you're off the drugs, in a good head-space, and when you're listening to my father, you're the best. You can be on the top of the money list in a year, but only if you stay out of your own way and you keep humble." Courtney left him sitting there to ponder his own thoughts while she made her way to her room to deal with the onslaught of emotions that having Jack so close produced.

This time, she'd keep those feelings to herself.

And she'd refrain from turning to the arms of an animal for comfort.

5

Jack crossed his legs, bent over, and reached for the ground, giving his back a good stretch. Every muscle in his body ached. Even his brain was sore from all the mental power he'd been exerting over the last few days. Rudy had a grueling schedule, worse than Jack remembered, and the hardest part was that Jack had hardly seen Courtney.

Every morning, Jack woke before the sun rose and went for a run. By the time he returned, he had barely enough time to shower before Rudy tossed a protein shake and a golf club at Jack, sending him to the driving range. Jack then spent the day doing whatever it was that Rudy told him to do until dinnertime, when all Jack wanted to do was take a hot bath and climb into bed and sleep for ten hours.

"Jack!" Bri yelled, skipping down the walkway from

the house to the driving range. Her blond curls bounced vigorously around her shoulders.

“Hey, runt.” He smiled. She was an incredible kid, so it was hard to believe she belonged to Rivers. “How was your day?”

“I’m five now.” She held up her hands, begging him to pick her up. “Today is my party. Mommy and Grandpa got off work early.”

“I know. They are letting me take some time off from my training.” He lifted her in the air, twirling her around. “Happy birthday. I have something for you.” He gave her a little hug and then set her on the grass.

She was so sweet and innocent, and she made him feel alive, but more importantly, loved. Amazing what kids can do for your health. Every time he looked at her, he knew he would do anything for the little girl. It just sucked that her father had to be such an asshole and a deadbeat.

“What! What!” She jumped up and down.

“Come on.” He took her hand and headed toward the house. “It’s upstairs. I finished it today, but don’t tell Mommy or Grandpa, because they will be mad. I was supposed to be swinging that club all day, and I just didn’t.” When he looked up, he stopped. Courtney stood by the door, arms folded, just staring at them. “So, my father lets you practice at home, and you play hooky.”

“Only for an hour and it was for a good cause, you’ll see,” he said.

Courtney shook her head. "This is how it starts," she said under her breath.

Jack let the statement go, for now. He wasn't about to say anything in front of a little girl.

Bri tugged at his hand.

"Let's go."

He squeezed her hand. "I'm coming."

"Gosh, you're slow." She giggled, tugging him faster. "I want my surprise!" She yanked him right past Courtney, who smiled at Bri but gave him an evil glare.

"Where is it?" Bri jumped up and down in front of him.

"Hold your horses, missy. Stay right here." He smiled, waving his finger in her cute little face. "I'll be right back." He jumped the stairs two at time, feeling like a little kid himself. It had been odd to learn a craft at his age, but he needed to make a few dollars, and carving things from wood and selling them on the street ended up being a decent way to live from one meal to the next when he wasn't working on a fishing boat charter.

It also gave him something to do while he detoxed his body.

"Come on up!" he called from the top of the stairs.

Both Bri and Courtney came dashing up the staircase, giggling like schoolgirls. It warmed his heart to see them both so happy with each other.

"Where?" Bri stood in front of him with her hands planted firmly on her hips, just like her mother. Her gaze darted around excitedly. "Where!" she begged.

"Right in there." Jack pointed to her room, then stepped aside, puffing out his chest. He hadn't done something that gave him any sense of pride in many years.

Bri ran into her room, then came to a crashing halt, dead center. "Mommy! Look!" Bri turned in a circle, smiling brightly and pointing to the dollhouse. "Mommy! It's a real house! Just like the one I showed you in the magazine, only better!"

"Oh, my." Courtney looked at the freshly painted dollhouse, with furniture and dolls. "Did you...how did you..."

"I built the house and bought the stuff that goes in it." Jack shrugged, stuffing his hands in his pockets, feeling a little stupid. "I saw that you and she were making a wish list for Christmas. I thought it would be a nice surprise."

"I love it." Bri dropped to her knees and immediately started playing. In a singsong voice, she had the little people talking to one another, and she moved them about the dollhouse.

"You shouldn't have." Courtney turned from him, wiping her cheeks. "But thank you. Bri, what do you say?"

"Huh? Oh, thanks, Jack. You're the best!" Bri jumped up, tugging at him to give him a kiss. "You gonna come to the party?"

"I wouldn't miss it." He smoothed her hair and smiled. "Go play." He nudged her, then turned to find Courtney had left.

Damn. Why'd he'd have to go and make her cry. Again.

Jack searched the house and finally found her in the kitchen. "I didn't mean to upset you. I just wanted to do something nice for Bri for her birthday."

Courtney jumped. Her tea sloshed out onto the counter.

"I didn't mean to scare you either," Jack said, pouring himself a cup of coffee.

She smoothed her jeans and looked at him. "You didn't upset me." A small smile appeared on her sad face. "You made her really happy. I can't believe you made that with your own hands. You weren't that handy five years ago."

"I wasn't a lot of things five years ago." He blew into the hot liquid and took a long sip, letting the bitter coffee give his body and his mind a good jolt.

"It was very sweet. Unfortunately, I'd been sending a list of things for Tom to get her, and a dollhouse was one of them." Courtney tucked her short blond hair behind her ears. "I'm afraid she's getting a little too attached to you."

"I'm kind of attached to the little runt myself."

"She's resilient, but it's been hard to balance this with Tom and all the disappointment she's faced with him. I could have easily lived on my own with her, but she needed stability in her life, especially when it came to a strong male figure." She twisted her tea bag around a spoon, then glanced up at him. "That's why I moved back here, and I don't want to see her get her heart ripped out when you leave."

"I don't plan on leaving," he said.

"That's funny, because you're here to train. Once you're ready, you'll be on tour, which means you'll leave."

"But I'll be back. I'm not going to disappear again."

"You don't know that." She patted the center of his chest. "I'm a grown-up now. I understand things in ways I couldn't when I was seventeen. She's a baby. And I can see the infatuation in her eyes. She idolizes you already. I can't risk her heart. She might be resilient, but she already has a father who jerks her around. We don't need another golfer coming in and out of her life."

He pounded the counter with his fist. "Damn it, Court. I didn't know how you felt until it was too late. I was scared and confused, young and stupid. There were things going on in my life that you didn't know about. We were all living a crazy life back then. I got caught up in—"

She held up her hand and took a deep breath. "You need to understand this doesn't have anything to do with you, or about how you hurt my feelings when I told you I cared about you all those years ago. This only has to do with Bri. I need to make sure my daughter has a stable and loving environment. Tom doesn't make that easy. And you're not helping, but it's not you. If my father had someone else in here training, she'd become attached to anyone who gave her that kind of attention."

"Oh," he said, letting out a long breath. "She's a great kid, and I'm just being nice."

"I know, but can we dial it down a notch? Maybe next time get her a doll and not the whole house?"

"I can do that." He nodded. "I want to ask you some questions about Tom, like why doesn't he have joint custody? Or visitation?"

"That was the deal when we got divorced."

Jack shook his head. "I don't understand a deal where a father walks away from his only child. I could never do that."

"This is none of your business, and I'd appreciate it if you stayed out of it."

"Living here makes it my business." He shook his head. "We used to be best friends; why won't you tell me what happened?"

Anger flickered behind her cool-blue eyes. "Because it's not your business."

"Perhaps not, but sometimes it helps to talk about things." Jack knew he shouldn't push so hard, but something told him what happened after he left got so much worse for Courtney.

"I have Nicole and my father for that." Courtney looked at her watch. "Bri, come on, it's time to go," she yelled toward the stairs. "Chuck E. Cheese is waiting."

"Yay!" Bri skipped into the kitchen carrying a couple of dolls and a little handbag. "Do you think Daddy is going to change his mind and come to my party? I wan't to tell him all about the new dollhouse Jack made me."

"I'm sorry, honey; he hasn't called me to tell me he'll be there," Courtney said.

Bri opened her purse and set her tiny dolls inside. She swiped at her cheeks. "Maybe he'll call on the way over. He changes his mind a lot."

Jack felt like his rock bottom just roared up and swallowed him. He would have to leave at some point. Courtney was right about that.

And he'd have to be more careful about the time he spent with darling little Bri.

"Thank you."

Courtney tossed a napkin over a half-eaten slice of pizza and stared at her father. "For what?"

"For being so patient with Jack."

"I have to give him credit. He's trying." She glanced across the room. Bri ran around with five other little girls while a couple mothers stood off in the background. Poor Jack hung out in the corner eating a ton of pizza and sipping on a soda.

He'd taken to heart what she'd said in the kitchen.

Maybe too much so because he'd barely interacted with the birthday girl since they'd left the house.

"You're still very reserved around him," her father said. "You don't trust him."

Her heart dropped to the bottom of her gut. She grabbed her father's hand. "Tom," she whispered.

"What?"

"Tom. He's outside." Her pulse hammered in her throat, constricting her airways. "And he's got a woman on his arm." The nerve of that man to bring his latest conquest to his daughter's birthday party.

"I think we might need to be more concerned about the last time Jack and Tom saw each other," her father said. "I think Tom's last words at court were *come near me or my family and I'll make sure you rot in prison.*"

"You don't think he still has the power to do that?" Courtney asked.

"The fact that he's not in jail for what he did to you, I'd say yeah." Her father stood and smoothed down the front of his slacks. "I'll go cut Tom off at the pass. You go distract Jack. I don't want anything ruining my granddaughter's birthday."

"Neither do I, but if Tom wants to see her, he can. You have to let him in. We'll just have to send Jack away."

Her father closed his eyes for a long moment before blinking them open. She knew it took a lot for him to remain composed when it came to Tom and letting him see Bri. "Tom is a criminal, and the only reason why I go along with this insanity is because I know he doesn't fight fair, and I do fear he'd take her from us and find a way to have you arrested."

"Well, let's make sure that doesn't happen." She

leaned in and kissed her father's cheek. "If necessary, I'll take Jack for a walk so Tom can see Bri."

"I hate this," her father muttered.

Not as much as she did, and while her ex-husband was a horrible person, she'd made her share of mistakes, one of which could cost her custody of her child, something she'd never let happen.

"Hey, you." She stood next to Jack and watched her daughter play in the bouncy house with her friends. "You've been really quiet since we got here."

"I've been thinking about my mom. I barely remember her," Jack said. "I was five when she died and fifteen when my dad passed, but they both loved me more than anything on this planet." He turned and faced her. "You and your father, you both love Bri. But Tom?" Jack jerked his head toward the front door. "Does he even know what the word means?"

Courtney rested her hand on Jack's shoulder. "Don't get mad at me for saying this, but do you?"

He nodded. "Yeah. Actually, I do." He raised his paper cup to his mouth and sucked on the straw. "Are you going to let him see her?"

"Excuse me?"

"I saw him outside, and I can't believe he still sees that woman. Are they an item?" Jack asked.

Courtney glanced over her shoulder. She couldn't really see Tom or her father. The woman, however, tapped her open-toed shoe right in front of the picture window, giving Courtney a good view. "I've never seen her."

"You're kidding, right? That's Tina."

"Tina? Who's Tina?"

Jack coughed and spit out some soda. "You really don't know who that is?"

She shook her head. "Should I?"

Jack ran a hand down his jaw, bringing his thumb and index finger together at the base of his chin.

"Who is she, Jack?"

"I think this is one of those things I should stay out of." He dared to take a few steps toward the back of the play area.

"Like hell. You're going to tell me who that is, or I'm going to march myself out there and find out for myself."

Jack chuckled. "You're not going to do that because you don't want to cause a scene on your daughter's birthday."

She groaned, resenting that Jack called her on her bullshit.

"I'll tell you, but I want some information in return."

"Fine," she mumbled. Curiosity had gotten the better of her. "What is it that you want to know?"

"Why do you have this deal with Tom that he has to set it up to see Bri ahead of time?"

"You know better than anyone that Tom had a taste for certain drugs and he got me hooked on them as well. When I left, he was going to use that to take Bri from me in order to try to force me to stay with him. In the end, because he doesn't want Bri, he agreed to give me full custody." She shrugged. "It's that simple."

"That doesn't answer my entire question."

Courtney let out a puff of air. There was no way she was going to tell Jack the whole truth. She'd barely been able to get through it all when she had to tell her father, and she swore, unless she was forced to, she'd never tell that story again. Finding out who that woman was didn't matter that much. "There are a lot of things about mine and Tom's divorce that are private and locked up in gag orders." She waved to Bri who jumped up and down in a circle before taking her best friend's hand and running up on the dancing stage. "I don't need to know who that woman is, but I do need to know that if Tom does end up coming in to say hello to his daughter, you will step away and not engage."

"I'll gladly hide in the back room. Anything not to see that man," Jack said, raising his cup. "I'll tell you who that woman is if you promise me you won't go running off half-cocked."

"So, she's one of the many he was sleeping with while on tour when we first married."

Jack nodded. "Remember the night Bri was born?"

"That's who he was with?"

"Your dad asked me to go find him when you went into labor. Sadly, I knew exactly where he was because I was at the same party and cheating on Wendy. It was a bad scene all around, and I think that night I realized what a mess I'd made of my life, and I knew if I didn't turn it around, something bad was going to happen, but the very next day I found myself doing the same insane thing."

"Yeah, and a year later, you whacked Tom in the back with your driver on national television."

"For the record. I absolutely regret doing that, but I don't regret telling him to F off."

The front door swished open. Courtney smiled as her father walked in, alone. "What did he want?" she asked.

"Not to see his daughter," her father said.

She clutched the pendant dangling from her neck. She promised herself, the longer this went on, the better off both she and Bri would be because eventually, what Tom held over her wouldn't matter anymore because she'd be able to prove she was a fit mother on all fronts.

"But he knew we were here, so why did he show his face?" Jack asked with disdain dripping from every syllable.

"He wants a rematch, and he wants it soon," Rudy said. "I told him I'd sign Jack up for the Randell Classic."

Jack dropped his soda. The lid flipped off, and the liquid went flying.

"You did what?" Courtney asked with a screechy voice. "Have you lost your flipping marbles?"

"Nope. And for the next few weeks we're not going to argue about it. You're just going to do it. Now, let's enjoy the rest of the birthday party."

6

Courtney sat in the waiting room of her doctor's office after her scheduled cat scan with her head behind a magazine. She'd read the same article three times now and still had no idea what it was about. Her leg rattled uncontrollably. Every time she made herself stop, her body started twitching again.

"Relax, would ya?" Jack said, patting her thigh and giving it a little squeeze.

She glared him. "I can't believe you agreed to come."

"It's not like Rudy gave me much of a choice." He threw his hands wide and tossed her a sheepish grin. "And after both of us tried to talk him out of me attending this tournament with Tom being there, and the way he acted, I thought it was best if I just did what he said."

"Because you can only think about yourself and your great comeback."

Jack laughed. "Right, because I'm playing so well right now."

"Maybe if you'd actually get out of your head and focus..." She shook her head. "I don't know why I bother. You're never going to listen or change."

"I can't win with you, can I?" Jack asked as he yanked the magazine from her hands. "I feel like that no matter what I do, how good our conversations are, we always end up with this negative dynamic, and I'm tired of it."

"Because you don't get it." She slumped in the horribly uncomfortable chair. "My father isn't going to kick you out or stop coaching you if you say no to him on certain things outside the scope of normal golf training. He's desperate to have you back in his life. But instead of understanding that, you're too wrapped up in your own need to get back in the limelight that you just say, 'sure, no problem, Rudy; I'd be happy to.' Well, for one, I'm tired of being in the center of this, and frankly, I can take care of myself." She closed her eyes. She could see the humor in his, and she heard the hilarity of it all in her voice, and she didn't want to join in. She wanted to be pissed for a little while longer.

"Did you ever think your dad is just worried about you?"

She chuckled. "Not about this."

"I don't know. Whatever this is seems like a big deal."

"Oh, please. I fall over once—"

"You had some dizziness the other day." He tapped her knee.

She looked into his green gems that had her melting like milk chocolate. "I have dizziness when I'm in the sun too long."

"How did you get a concussion in the first place?"

She inhaled sharply. It was as if she could hear the metal smack into the back of her skull. The irony of Tom hitting her with a golf club smacked her right between the eyes. But it was only one of many beatings that she had to endure before she finally had the courage to leave.

"Shit," Jack mumbled, running a hand over his face and shaking his head. "He did this to you, didn't he?"

A woman with a clipboard entered the waiting room. "Courtney Wade," she announced.

Courtney stood, ignoring Jack as best she could and followed the nurse into the hallway toward an exam room.

Jack was two steps behind her.

"What the hell, Jack? No way. You have to leave."

"Give me a break, Courtney. Your dad told me I had to. Threatened to pull the plug on our so-called arrangement."

"You know that's bullshit. I just explained that to you."

"I'll leave the door open." The nurse looked skeptical, but she left Courtney there with the red-haired giant.

"What the hell is my father up to?" she muttered. "Is

he expecting you to give him a full report? Does he not believe me now? Tell me, Jack. What the hell is going on because this is ridiculous, and I can't believe we're both letting him be a puppet master like this." Her rant really wasn't for Jack to hear, much less answer. It was all rhetorical. She stood by the door, holding the handle. "Just leave."

"I'm not going to do that." Jack had the audacity to curl his fingers over hers. "I made a million and one mistakes when I was on tour in my early twenties. I was fucking up long before I fired your father, mostly because I wouldn't do things his way. I think this is his way of making sure I've changed." Jack stretched out on one of the chairs in the exam room. "And yes, I'm being selfish. I want back in the game, but I'm not lying about it. Or manipulating you. Or doing anything underhanded, so please, can we just humor the man?"

"What the hell does it look like I'm doing?" Courtney joined him, sitting on the other chair. "But I don't have to like it, and I don't like you playing in a tournament with Tom."

"Ah, so that's what this is really all about." Jack leaned forward and rested his elbows on his knees. He stared into her eyes with a soft, caring gaze. He always had this sweetness about him, even when he'd been behaving like an asshole. But that's what concerned her. The closer they got to the upcoming match, the more anxiety tickled her soul. Tom didn't come all the way to their daughter's party to inform them he wanted to play Jack and then didn't even bother to say hello to his little girl if he hadn't planned on at least trying to get in Jack's head.

Courtney couldn't believe it wasn't working.

"Aren't you worried about being in the same space with him?" Courtney asked.

"I might not even have to see him," Jack said. "I'll be one of the first tee times, and he'll be one of the last. So, stop worrying so much."

She wanted to argue some more, but the doctor meandered down the hallway.

"Ms. Wade." The doctor nodded, then stopped and arched a brow as he looked at Jack.

"Hey, Doctor Mills, meet my new bodyguard."

Jack chuckled. "Her father thought I should drive her today."

"Oh, really?" The doctor set a tablet on the counter. "I thought we just had a few dizzy spells while golfing."

"That's all it is," Courtney said. "My father is being a whackadoodle, as usual."

"You're father's a good man, Courtney." The doctor pulled out her X-rays and latest brain scan. "Everything looks fine. I don't see anything that would be causing you any problems. I bet you're letting yourself get dehydrated in this weather."

Courtney enjoyed giving Jack a smug look. "That's exactly what I told my dad."

"Increase your fluid intake and try to stay out of the sun for prolonged periods of time. I know that's impossible, though, so just make sure you're wearing a hat. If it gets worse, contact me immediately. Schedule another appointment for about three months, but as I've told you before, you may have this problem for the rest of your life. Just be aware of what triggers it and try to avoid those situations."

"I guess I'll need a new bodyguard then." Courtney stood, wanting to laugh at the look on the doctor's face. "Thanks, Doc. I appreciate it."

"No problem. Say hello to your dad."

"Will do." She hightailed it out of the office building, Jack following two steps behind.

"Why do you think your father had me come out here with you?" Jack leaned against the driver's side door.

"I'm guessing he's trying to get you out of your head since your game is way off, and it's his way of keeping an eye on both of us."

"Does…um…he know?" He took her hands in his and pulled her to his chest.

"Know what?" She balanced herself against his shoulders, knowing she should step away, but it felt too good to be in his arms.

"Did you ever tell him about us?" He rested his hands on her hips. His thumbs slipped under her shirt and rubbed tiny circles on her skin, sending heat to all her erogenous zones.

"There was never an us." Courtney blinked, switching her gaze toward the bright sun.

"There was almost an us. If the circumstances and timing had been different, there could have been an us. I know I wanted there to be an us."

Courtney opened her mouth, but the only noise that came out sounded more like a dying cow than anything else. She cleared her throat. "You never even gave me a second thought."

"That's not true." He pressed his lips against hers in a tender but passionate kiss. "I struggled with my feelings for you the day you turned sixteen. I was a grown man, and you were a child. It made me feel bad, and I did everything I could think of to make it go away, including sleeping with Wendy, but it didn't help."

"So, now are you going to blame me for her? Are you going to next tell me that you started snorting cocaine because of me?"

He shook his head. "No, sweetheart. You're missing the point. Don't you ever wonder what might have happened if I never married Wendy?"

"Every day. But you did marry her, and I married Tom, had his kid, and here we are now." She flattened her hand against the center of his chest and pushed. "But I never wonder if we would have ever ended up together because I know deep down that would have never happened because I couldn't give you what you wanted."

"And what is it you think I wanted back then?"

"Fame and fortune."

He cupped her chin. "That's where you're wrong." He stepped to the side and opened the driver's side door. "Sure. I wanted that to a certain extent. What tour golfer doesn't? But there are things that were going on in my life that you have no idea about, and had I not been dealing with them that night, I would have taken you home and into my bed, so don't go telling me what I was thinking when you told me how you felt." He slipped behind the steering wheel and slammed the door.

Courtney leaned against the doorjamb between the kitchen and family room, staring at her father sitting on the sofa with the family photo album on his lap. "What are you doing?" She sat down next to him on the living room couch.

"Just being nostalgic," her father said as he flipped through the pages. He tapped at an image of himself in a tux at his wedding. "Your mother was already pregnant. While getting married wasn't the smartest thing I'd ever done, I've never regretted marrying your mom or the time we spent together." He rubbed the picture of his wife with his thumb. "I did love her."

"I know some of that feeling." She helped him turn the page. "Though, I didn't love Tom, and I do regret marrying him. I really do, Dad. I know I sometimes say things that make it sound like my marriage had good moments, when it didn't. And while Tom was never a good husband and probably won't ever be a good father, he's still a human being, and Bri loves him."

Her father nodded. "I know. It kills me to admit that."

Courtney came across a picture of herself when

she'd been maybe two years old. "I'm amazed at how much Bri, minus the curls, looks like me." Courtney laughed.

"I'm amazed at how beautiful you both are, considering who your fathers are. I mean, I'm nothing to look at, and we both know I wasn't the best father."

"Dad." She cocked an eyebrow. "You're very handsome, and I wouldn't want anyone else helping me raise my daughter."

"You have to say that." He chuckled, flipping through the pages. "Jack's mother was a real knockout. Everyone wanted to date her."

"Her hair was so red."

"You used to think she was *The Little Mermaid,*" her father said with a lightness to his voice that he hadn't had in a while. "Jackson's eyes were emerald green. They made quite a pair. I miss them both so much." Rudy paused, looking at Courtney with admiration spilling from his loving gaze. "How's your mother?"

Courtney gasped.

"I know you've talked with her a few times. It doesn't bother me. She gave birth to you; ultimately she gave me the best thing I've ever had the pleasure of loving."

"In part, she's why I keep holding out on Tom. She never wanted to be a mother, but in my adult life, she's found a place for me, and I'm okay with that."

"I'm glad," Courtney's father said. "I have no ill will toward her."

"Do you have any regrets?" Courtney asked.

"Just one."

"Jack?"

"If you're gonna put it that way, I have two regrets." He cupped her face. "I belittled what you felt for him back then. I pushed you away from him."

She shook her head. "He did that all by himself. He married Wendy, knowing I cared about him. His choice. Besides, I can't regret being with Tom."

"Courtney Elizabeth." Rudy frowned. Tom was a lowlife, not worthy of anything.

"May not have the brightest thing I'd ever done, but he gave me the best thing I've ever had. Bri." She cocked a brow.

"Ouch." Her father tapped his chest.

"Truth sucks, don't it, Dad." She kissed his cheek. "Why'd you make Jack come with me today?"

"The truth?"

Courtney nodded.

"Besides the fact that he's falling apart at the seams and I wanted to give him a break, he's been driving me nuts with questions about your condition. I figured it was the only way to get him off my back and realize that you're just fine. Just have to listen to the doctor more. He told you to make sure you drank lots of water, not…" He held up her soda. "Diet Coke."

"Oh, come on. One isn't going to kill me, and it's liquid."

"I'll get you some water." Rudy stood, then held up his hand when she went to protest. "Humor the old man." He winked.

Courtney continued to look through the family photo album. Her mother never really looked happy in any of the images. And while she hadn't seen her mother since she walked out on them, she had talked with her numerous times. Her mother said she'd be willing to be her friend, but she was no mother.

Courtney had to agree. Her mother was immature and incapable of taking care of another soul, but she wanted to have her in her life, even if by phone. "Oh, my." She looked at a picture of a young teenaged Jack, standing next to prepubescent Courtney. "What a geek."

"I was never a geek." Jack chuckled, settling on the sofa next to her.

"Where's Bri?" Courtney scowled.

"She found Grandpa in the kitchen with an ice cream scoop." He pulled the album onto his lap. "I don't look like a geek at all."

"Not you, me. Look at how dorky I was back then."

"I thought you were cute." He tapped the picture.

She giggled. "And I thought you were the cat's meow."

He meowed.

She rolled her eyes.

"Mommy!" Bri bounced in the room, breaking the tension that had begun to build.

Courtney opened her arms.

Bri jumped on Courtney's lap, brushing back her hair.

"I think it's time we get a haircut," Courtney

commented, running her fingers through Bri's long curls.

"You mean like Jack?" Bri asked innocently.

"Excuse me?" Jack tilted his head. "I don't need a haircut."

"Gosh, grown-ups are so silly. That's because you already had one." Bri tapped his shoulders. "It used to be down to here." She cupped Jack's face. "And you used to have a big scruffy beard."

Courtney felt her heart leap from her chest; her pulse pounded so hard she could feel her temple pump. "Bri, honey. What makes you say that?"

Bri rubbed his cheeks with his palms. "I have a picture of it."

Courtney swallowed.

"You do?" Jack asked.

"Mommy has the picture too."

Courtney coughed. "Bri, let's go get ready for bed."

"What picture? Can you show me this picture, Bri?" Jack's gaze darted from Bri to Courtney. His green gems were unrelenting and unforgiving.

"I can." Bri jumped to her feet and pulled Jack by the hand. "Thursday nights when Mommy went out with Nicole, Grandpa had his poker buddies over, and sometimes they would talk about you. Sometimes Nicole and Mommy would talk about you."

"Bri, this isn't the time for this, and you must have him mistaken for someone else," Courtney said behind a clenched jaw. "I'm sure Jack has something else he needs to do right now."

"Nope, been looking at pictures anyway. I'd like to see this one." His smile didn't hide his anger.

"Where did you get this picture?" Courtney took Bri in her arms.

"I'm sorry, Mommy." Bri's lip quivered. "Please don't be mad at me. I wanted a picture of…him." She looked at Jack and then stuffed her face in Courtney's neck and cried.

Now Courtney felt like a heel. But Bri had been told before to stay out of Mommy's things, and she had to learn that some things were private. "I'm disappointed, baby. I've told you before. You should've just asked me." Courtney rubbed her back, looking at Jack, pleading with him to drop it.

He blinked, then turned, shoving his hands deep in his pockets.

"I'm sorry, Mommy. But Jack seemed important, and I wanted to know him."

"Can I see the picture?" Jack asked.

"I'll give it back to you, Mommy. I promise."

"Go ahead." Courtney put her daughter down and patted her behind. "Go get it."

Bri smiled and ran for the stairs.

Courtney didn't look at Jack. She couldn't. The faint homey smell from the candle she lit earlier soothed her fear but did nothing to hide her shame. She'd spied on him. How horrible was that? "I don't think it's a good idea to give her a picture." Courtney turned and faced him. "She's way too attached as it is."

"I know how she feels," Jack said. "I've done my best to keep her at arm's length."

"Thank you. I do appreciate it."

"Does she really have a picture of me that you took in the last couple of years?" Jack asked.

"I just wanted to know you were okay, that's all. You disappeared off the face of the earth after the... Well, my father and I were worried."

Much to her surprise he palmed her cheek. "Thank you," he whispered. "It's nice to know you actually thought about me."

"You're not mad?"

"I didn't say that." He smiled, and his eyes softened. "I feel slightly invaded, but I also feel like you never stopped caring."

Courtney didn't know what to think or how to feel right now. "My father doesn't know I found out where you were last year, and I don't want him to know."

"Yes, I do, did." Rudy waltzed into the room with Bri in his arms.

"Here." Bri shoved the picture of a bearded, long-haired, red-headed hippy in Jack's face. "I like you better now." Bri touched his face. "When you kiss me good night, it's soft. I bet that thing would be all scratchy."

Jack chuckled.

Courtney stood there, stunned, unable to react to anything. "You knew?" she asked her father.

"I hired the same P.I."

"What?" Jack asked.

"Bri, go play with your dollhouse for a little while. Looks like you get to stay up a bit later tonight," Grandpa said.

"Okay!" Bri skipped off to her room as if she hadn't a care in the world.

Courtney rubbed her temples. A wave of dizziness washed over her. "We paid for that info twice?"

"No." Rudy laughed. "I went to hire him right before he gave you those pictures. I saw them before you." Rudy turned to Jack. "I prayed you'd come home." Rudy pulled Jack close, giving him a big bear hug. "I've been waiting for your return."

Pangs of jealousy flowed through Courtney's veins. The son her father never had but always adored. When Jack's father died, Rudy took him in and gave most of his attention to the All-American boy, Jackson Albert Hollister. She swore her son would never be named that.

Not that it mattered. A relationship with Jack back then had been a fantasy. A relationship with Jack today, impossible. It didn't matter that she'd probably always love him. And where were these thoughts coming from? She was mad, hurt, confused. Hell, she didn't know what she was.

"I can't believe you both went looking for me."

"We were worried. You're family to us." Rudy placed a fatherly hand on Jack's shoulder.

"I need to go give Bri a bath," Courtney said, in no mood to deal with the emotions swirling around in her mind and heart. "We've got a busy day tomorrow."

Her father curled his fingers around her biceps. "I love you."

"I love you, too, Dad." She glanced at Jack who continued to stare at the picture of himself while he scratched at the sides of his face. "Good night, Jack."

"Sleep well, Courtney."

Sleep wouldn't come easily, and when it did, it would be filled with dreams of Jack.

7

Jack sat on the edge of his bed holding the image Bri had given him. It had been taken maybe a little over a year ago. He'd been off the cocaine for a few months. He'd been working on a fishing charter boat while learning how to build things out of wood. The picture was taken in front of the trailer park he lived in while he sat at the entrance selling one of his latest masterpieces.

In a few short years, he'd gone from having millions in the bank to wondering why he even bothered having a checking account.

"Hey," Courtney said softly. She stood in the doorway of his bedroom wearing a long T-shirt and a pair of boxers. "Are you okay?"

"I'm still in shock."

"Imagine what it was like for me when I saw you with all that hair." She waved her fingers at the top of her shoulders. "You have great hair, but it looks much better shorter and damn, that beard. That was a bit much. If I had seen you in the street, I'm not sure I would have recognized you."

"That was kind of the point." He set the image on the nightstand, snagging his beer. "I know I shouldn't be having this, but I needed to take the edge off."

She reached for it, lifting it to her lips. "I don't blame you. It's been a strange turn of events lately."

"You can say that again." He took the bottle back and finished the last swig. He fluffed his pillow and stretched out on the bed, crossing his ankles. Tears stung at his eyes. When he'd returned, he knew they could easily reject him. Hell, he expected both Rudy and Courtney to tell him to take a hike. Jack figured he'd have to spend days, maybe even a week convincing them to work with him. If Rudy said no after that, Jack would have to decide if he had the balls to go it alone.

But he never expected either one of them would go looking for him.

Talk about being humbled.

"Have a seat." He patted the mattress.

"Can I ask you a question?" She made herself comfortable next to him, pulling one of the throw pillows across her lap.

"Of course." He could feel the warmth from her body float off her skin and land on his like a blanket of hot soapy water.

"Actually, it's a series of questions."

"I'll do my best to answer honestly."

She nodded. "You stormed off the golf course after hitting Tom and the press found you—"

"That's so very well documented. You really want to know the sordid details?"

"Well, you left the course and went on a bender. You were arrested. You spent a few days in jail. You went to court. You were found guilty and were sentenced to community service."

"Ah." He laced his fingers through hers and stared at their intertwined hands. "You want to know how I disappeared."

"You and Wendy had already separated. Her father had dropped you."

There were so many moments Jack wished he could change. One would have been the night that Courtney told him that she loved him. One of the others would have been when he found out the truth about Wendy's pregnancy. Had he known that, he might not have ended up having to watch Tom marry and have a child with the one woman that made Jack feel alive. "I took what I had left and begged the judge to let me serve out my sentence anywhere but here. He sent me to Galveston. I continued to act like an asshole for a while, meaning I continued to do drugs and try to kill myself slowly with them. Then, and I really don't know what changed, but I got tired of being tired all the time. I quit the drugs, took up woodworking, got a job, and turned things around. Eventually, I picked up a golf club and started practicing, and then I ended up back here."

"What happened between you and Wendy?"

He laughed. "What didn't happen with us? We were a match made in hell, that's for damn fucking sure."

"You and I stopped being close the night you told me to go home to daddy. I'm curious as to why you left her when you told me she was your soul mate."

"First off, I lied about that," he admitted, but he wasn't sure he was ready to tell her the entire truth, in part, because he wasn't sure she would be willing to tell him everything about Tom. Not that he needed tit for tat, but they each used their spouses to hurt the other. That he knew to be the truth. "The only thing she ever was to me was a direct path to an ulcer."

Courtney laughed. "Sorry."

"Don't be. I know I made a mistake by marrying her. I only wish it had been my idea to get a divorce."

"You didn't leave her?"

He shook his head. God, how he hated to admit this to Courtney. All it did was show how weak and driven by greed, fame, and shame he was. From the second he'd gone to bed with Wendy, he'd started a downward spiral that he wasn't sure he'd ever be able to stop. At one point, he couldn't even look himself in the eye, much less Rudy and his beautiful daughter. "I stopped towing the line, and she gave me an ultimatum."

"You don't do those well," Courtney said. "I'll be honest. I told my dad that all these rules he's been putting on you would backfire."

Jack shifted to his side and let his gaze soak in the sexy woman sprawled out next to him. She'd been a spitfire of a teenager. Smart, energetic, and she always had a way of making him feel as though he could do and be anything. That used to scare the crap out of him. A teenager shouldn't make a grown man feel that way. And the older she got, the more he noticed her and more he pushed her and her father away.

It was more than his growing attachment to Courtney that had Jack driving down the wrong road. He'd become impatient with Rudy's plan for his career. Jack didn't want to wait. He wanted it all, and he wanted it all right now.

"I've broken out in hives at least a dozen times in the last couple of weeks since moving into this house, and I have a to-go bag packed and ready to sneak out in the middle of the night."

"That's really not funny, but I understand. My dad can be intense."

"You don't have to tell me that. When I first went pro, I thought I'd never be able to live up to his standards."

"Back then, I'm not sure either of us could live up to what he thought we should be doing. He's changed a lot since then. I think he's really trying not to pile on the pressure, but at the same time, he doesn't want to be soft on you either."

"I know I've let him down."

"I can't believe I'm going to say this, but he let you down too."

Jack snapped his gaze from their intertwined fingers to her sweet blue orbs. "I don't see how you could say that. He's been nothing but wonderful to me my entire life, and all I did was shit on him and the memory of my parents."

She cupped his cheek. "Not entirely true."

He chuckled. "But you're not denying it completely."

"Of course not. We were both brats," she said. "But, for me, my father had had certain expectations that I struggled to live up to, and one of them was being second to you."

Jack arched a brow. "What the hell does that mean?"

"You were the son he never had, and he wanted you to be number one."

"He had big dreams for you too." Jack understood the kind of pressure Rudy put on all the golfers he worked with. He'd seen it firsthand while still in high school on the varsity team and watching Rudy work with some of the best golfers in the world.

Jack had helped destroy Rudy's reputation and while Rudy still had a lucrative pro shop, he no longer worked with golfers on tour. That was in part Jack's fault.

"Of course, he did, but his focus was on you."

"Were you jealous?" he asked.

She patted the side of his face before dropping her hand to her side. "Never of you, but sometimes I would feel a little envious of how proud my dad was of you and he'd boast about your future."

"Until I started fucking it up, which wasn't too far after it started."

She laughed. "You were getting a chip on your shoulder long before you started dating Wendy."

Oh boy, had he ever. Money and fame had gone to his head in ways he hadn't ever expected. He had no idea the price of admission would be his self-confidence. The higher up on the money list he got, the more friends showed up at his doorstep. Only they weren't friends.

They were people who wanted a piece of him, and they all took what they wanted until Jack had nothing left to give.

If he ever had anything to begin with.

He remembered the very first time he tried cocaine. It had been with, of all people, Tom and Wendy. He'd been twenty-three, and the realization of how good he had it hit him hard. The pressure of always being at the top of his game weighed heavy on his shoulders. So heavy, he needed something to take the edge off, and a little booze and a romp in the sack with a good-looking lady wasn't cutting it anymore.

Wendy and Tom opened up a world of adrenaline that Jack thought only existed on the golf course, and from there, Jack went down a path that most never came back from.

"I really have changed, Courtney."

"I know you have," she said. "The question is will that change stick when the pressure is poured on when you get back on tour."

Courtney hated reminding Jack that being out on tour could pull all his demons to the surface, but she wanted him to be as prepared as possible. She hoped he really had put the past where it belonged, and she in turned owed it to herself, and to him, to do the same.

"I'd be lying if I said I wasn't absolutely terrified about playing in a tournament, especially one where Tom is going to be there."

"You don't worry about him at all. He'll try to get in your head, but don't let him. Play your game. And play smart. It's a local tournament, so we'll be right there supporting you."

"You'll go? Walk the lines?"

"Yes. I'll be there," she said.

"I really do appreciate that." He lay on his side with his head cradled in his hand. "My game is all over the place."

"I know. You've got to get out of you head and stop thinking about it. Just pretend you're playing me."

"I wish it were that simple. The newspapers and golf channels are already talking about me being at the Randall Classic. They want interviews, and they are speculating why I'm not giving them."

"I agree with my father on his plan to ease you back into the limelight. Just stick with the script. You'll be okay."

"Is that why you came in here? To give me a little pep talk?"

Why had she entered his room? Her heart beat erratically. She couldn't fill her lungs with enough oxygen. She became painfully aware that she was lying in his bed while they were both in their pajamas.

At least the door was open.

Or was that a good thing?

He tilted her chin with his thumb and forefinger. "What's going on in that pretty little head of yours?"

"Not much, trust me."

"Are you thinking about this?" He leaned in and kissed her. His tongue slipped between her lips, probing the inside of her mouth like a missile in search of its target.

A guttural groan built deep in the pit of her stomach. It bubbled from her gut to the back of her throat. Without thinking, she wrapped her arms around his broad shoulders, leaning into his strong chest, deepening the kiss.

His hands roamed her body, squeezing her ass as he smoothed down the back of her leg, lifting it up over his.

She enjoyed the way his tender lips dotted kisses down the side of her neck and under her earlobe.

"Mommy?"

"Oh shit," Jack whispered, practically jumping off the bed. He tripped on something and tumbled to the floor.

"Are you okay?" Bri raced to his side, dropping to her knees.

"Yup." Jack sat cross-legged on the floor, leaning against the wall.

"What are you doing out of bed, baby?" Courtney quickly made sure all of her clothing was where it was supposed to be before lifting Bri up and setting her on her lap.

"I wanted some water, and I thought I heard you talking," Bri said, brushing her unruly locks from her face. "But you were kissing instead." She giggled.

Wonderful. This was the last thing she needed her daughter to see, much less talk about, and that's exactly what five-year-old little girls would do. "Why don't we go get that water and tuck you back in."

"Can Jack do it?" Bri asked.

"I think it's best if Mommy does it tonight." Jack stood and kissed Bri's forehead. "I'll see you for breakfast."

"Okay," Bri said.

Courtney stood, hiking Bri up on her hip. She was getting too big to carry like this. "Say good night to Jack."

"Night, Jack." Bri waved.

"Night, kiddo," Jack said. "Good night, Courtney."

Courtney nodded. Quietly, she tiptoed down the hallway toward the bathroom. "I know Mommy said secrets were bad, but let's not tell anyone you saw me kissing Jack, okay?"

"Did you like it?" Bri asked while she fiddled with the water faucet in the bathroom.

Oh, what a loaded question. "I did," she admitted.

"And you like Jack, right?"

"Of course, I do," Courtney said.

Bri set her water glass on the counter and turned and stared at Courtney. "Then why don't you want anyone to know?"

"Grown-ups are complicated, baby. But mostly because Jack has that big tournament coming up, and I don't want him to have any distractions."

Bri lifted her hand and nodded as if she totally understood. "Grandpa and his no hanky panky rule before matches."

Courtney covered her mouth. "Do you know what hanky panky means?"

Bri pursed her lips. "Duh, Mommy. It's what you and Jack were just doing. I'm five now. I know these things."

"Being such a big girl then, you understand that kissing is a private thing."

Bri took her mother's hand and marched them into her bedroom. She jumped up into her bed and pulled up the covers. "Then next time you might want to close the door. But I won't say anything." Bri lowered her chin. "Unless asked, because lying is a bad thing."

"That's true, and I wouldn't expect you to lie, not about that or anything to anyone." Courtney gave her little girl a big hug and kiss. "I love you, baby." As quietly as possible, she slipped into her room and closed the door.

Her phone buzzed on the nightstand.

Jack: Hanky panky? You are so in trouble when she's a teenager.

Courtney: This is why she won't be allowed to date golfers.

Jack: By the way, I liked it too.

Courtney: Do you always listen in on other people's conversations?

Jack: When they pertain to me, absolutely. Good night, Courtney. No hanky panky until after the match.

No hanky panky again, ever.

But she'd wait to tell him that until after the match. No need to get in his head and make things harder for him on the course.

Jack gritted his teeth and gripped his five iron, his least favorite club. As a matter of fact, he avoided using it as if it were the plague.

"Too much sway," Rudy said, giving him a gentle tap with a club in the knee. "Keep the lower body still."

"I thought I was," Jack mumbled as he steadied his hips. He lifted his gaze, eyeing the pin, only all he could think about was Courtney and her damned glorious lips and how they felt against his. Or the way she felt pressed against his chest. Or the way she smiled at him. Or the way she smelled like a strawberry field on a warm summer morning.

"Earth to golfer boy," Rudy said with a chuckle.

"Huh?" Jack took a step back.

"You left me for a while."

"Did not. I'm taking your correction." Jack addressed the ball, skulling his five iron and hitting the second worse shot of his life. The first one had been two balls ago when he hit the heel of the club, sending the ball completely in the wrong direction.

"Listen, boy. You have your first tournament this weekend, and right now, Bri can swing better than you."

"Bri can do anything better than me," Jack said under his breath. "She even said so earlier."

But his observation caught a hearty laugh from Rudy. "She calls them like she sees them." Rudy smiled proudly.

Jack couldn't help it. He glanced over his shoulder. Bri sat in her tire swing, pumping her legs wildly while Courtney stood behind her, barely pushing. "She's a great kid." Jack brought his attention back to hitting the ball. "Maybe you should focus on her game and give up on me all together."

Rudy's strong father hand came down on his shoulder. "I know you're scared, son. So am I. But the only thing standing in your way right now is the gray matter between your ears. Clear you mind and get in the zone. Whatever it takes, just do it."

He eyed Courtney who nodded and smiled as if she could hear the conversation. Whatever was brewing between them had been there for years. It wasn't anything new, and he'd been not dealing with it, for as long as he could remember.

Maybe it was time to deal with the emotions that swirled around in his heart and soul when it came to Courtney. Maybe if he admitted to himself that he cared about her, really genuinely cared, he could get her out from under his skin.

"I care about Courtney," he whispered.

Rudy coughed. "What?"

Jack smiled. "Nothing." He swung. "Damn." He watched the arch of the ball. "Okay." He raised his fist in the air as the ball bounced two feet from the pin.

"When you step up to the tee box this weekend, I wouldn't say those words out loud." Rudy folded his arms and puffed out his chest. "Besides the cameras picking it up, we have no idea what kind of taunting game Tom will be up to, and we know he'll be up to something."

"Jesus. Why the hell did you have to remind me of that?" Jack stepped away from the bucket of balls. "That doesn't help my headspace."

"Well, you're gonna have to face him sooner or later on the golf course, so you need to mentally prepare yourself. So is Courtney, since she's going to be your caddy."

"Like fucking hell!" The thought of Courtney having to be anywhere near Tom made him wish he had knocked the sucker out four years ago. "She won't do it."

"Actually, I will." Courtney stood behind him. "Please watch the language around Bri."

"What should I watch it do?" Jack said sarcastically, looking around in search for the child, who seemed to have disappeared in the last few minutes.

"She's in the sandbox, but she gets afraid when people swear. Tom and I did it a lot during the divorce," Courtney said in a calm mom voice. "Not to mention, she looks up to you."

"I look up to her." Jack rounded his shoulders, trying to inch the tension out. "Can we skip this tournament? I'm not ready."

"No. We can't. Just a way to wet your feet." Rudy slapped his back. "I'm gonna go play with Bri. Fix his swing." Rudy kissed Courtney and walked away.

Jack stood there and stared at her for what seemed like an eternity before he finally broke the mounting tension. "Not sure I can face Tom without ringing his neck."

"You'll have to wait in line. I spoke to him today."

"Why?" Jack muttered while he stretched out his aching back.

"He was pretending to ask about Bri's plans for the weekend since he'll be here, but he really wanted to know our plans." She handed him his club. "I didn't tell him anything, and then he mentioned he probably wouldn't have time to see Bri, even if I let him."

"He's a dick." Jack addressed the ball, and for the first time in about two days, he hit it square.

"Damn." Courtney lined up another one for him. "Was that his head?"

"No, his manhood." Jack smiled when she smiled back at him.

"He doesn't have much of a manhood." She laughed, waving her pinky at Jack.

"Gross, way too much info." He hit a few more balls, feeling like he was finally where he belonged.

With Courtney.

He hit balls for another hour and then spent two chipping and putting. By the end of the day, he was dead dog-tired.

He dropped down behind his favorite tree with a Gatorade, and he stared at the stars. He had to find a way to control himself around Tom. It wasn't just Courtney he felt the need to defend and protect. There was Bri. Beautiful, delightful, spunky little Bri. She stole his heart.

"Hey, you," Courtney said as she made herself comfortable next to him.

"Is Bri asleep?"

"She's in bed, slightly wired tonight, but Grandpa will deal with her if she gets up." Courtney smiled at him with her blue eyes shining against the hollow of the moon. "She's torn between wanting to watch me caddy for you or watch her father play."

"What about you?" His heart skipped a beat. A combination of rage and self-doubt filled his mind. Not a good mix for his game, or his temper.

Courtney laughed. "You have to ask? Of course, I'd rather caddy for you."

"And what about the hanky panky?" He leaned a little closer.

She cupped his face. "I like you, Jack. You know that. I've always cared a great deal for you, but that kiss was a mistake. You need to focus on your game, and I need to work on getting my life back on track."

"I see." He leaned back against the tree, releasing her hand. "And you're right." He had to accept the fact that this ship has sailed.

8

Jack couldn't remember ever being this nervous. Not even the first time he'd made the cut or the first time he'd made the tour.

He needed to calm his nerves.

This round, and his career, depended on his ability to stay cool under pressure.

He glanced at Courtney as she pulled into the parking lot of the golf course. He was happy that they had come to an understanding. They were still friends, and he had to admit, she still knew his game better than he did. He just hoped his sudden case of the jitters didn't make him look like a fool.

"Knock it off." She touched his bouncing leg as she put the vehicle into park.

"Sorry," he muttered, getting out of the passenger seat of her SUV.

"Jack." She touched his arm when he started to pull his clubs onto his back. "I'm supposed to do that."

"Oh." He didn't have a clue as to what he was doing. "Shit." He saw Tom talking with a bunch of reporters. "That's not good."

"Just ignore him." Courtney tugged at his biceps. "He's not on our radar, or our problem."

"I'm worried about the reporters." He had forgotten they'd be here, and he wasn't prepared to deal with them.

"Don't take this personally, but other than the first tee box shot, they aren't interested. Besides, Dad took care of most of them. They promised to leave you alone, unless you do something stupid." She squeezed his arm.

He patted her hand. "And if you do something stupid?" he asked, trying to lighten his own mood.

"Bri will spank me," she teased.

Jack kept his gaze on her as they passed Tom. He could feel him staring, but he needed to get inside the club and inside the men's locker room. "You can't come in with me." He stared blankly at her. "You're a woman."

"Really, I hadn't noticed."

"Well, isn't this like old times?" Tom asked as he approached. "I heard you dusted off your caddy digs. But for the likes of this washed-up drug addict? Really, Courtney, you can do better."

Jack opened and closed his fists while he clenched

his jaw, reminding himself that engaging with this asshole wouldn't be a good idea.

"I don't know. He's a step up from you," Courtney said.

The corners of Jack's mouth tipped into a slight smile. He pressed his hand on the small of Courtney's back.

"Take your hand off my wife." Tom puffed out his chest and inched closer.

If Jack were his old self, he'd either plant a wet one on Courtney's lips or get into a pissing match with Tom. But this was the new and improved Jack.

"Um, I'm your ex-wife," Courtney said with a sweet smile. "And if I want his hands on me, you have no opinion about the matter."

"I have lots of opinions." Tom leaned in. "And you don't want me to express them."

"Don't threaten me, Tom." Courtney stiffened her spine, standing up taller.

Jack's pulse raced. A bead of perspiration banded across his hairline. He wanted to run as far from the golf course as he could possibly get, snag a few cold beers and a fishing line, then stare at a body of water for hours doing absolutely nothing with his mind or his muscles.

He wanted to be anywhere but standing in a hallway with Tom, wanting to knock out one of his perfectly pearly-white straight teeth.

"Sweetheart, it's not a threat." Tom adjusted his belt,

widening his stance as if he were ready for a fight. "Where's Bri?"

Jack bit back a growl. He hated the way Bri's name rolled out of Tom's mouth. How could such a sweet little girl belong to such a monster?

"With her grandfather." Courtney tilted her head and grabbed Jack's hand and squeezed, hard. "You told me you wouldn't have time this weekend. You need to give me more than twenty-four hours' notice for visitation."

"Actually, I don't," Tom said. "I handed you physical custody because I'm a nice guy, but I'm still Bri's father."

Jack burst out laughing. He raised his free hand. "Sorry. I told myself a funny joke."

Tom narrowed his eyes. "After the match, we need to talk. Privately."

Jack stepped closer and cleared his throat. "Besides being busy, Courtney won't be spending time with you alone. You've got something to say, you'll say it in front of me or her father."

"Who the fuck do you think you are?" Tom held up both hands and took a step back. "You don't have a say in anything that has to do with my family."

"Right, because you're such an excellent dad. As a matter of fact, I think you're going to be named father of the year." Jack shook his hand free from Courtney and stepped in front of her. He'd had about enough of Tom, and he wasn't going to stand there and listen to his bullshit. How he wished he had the proof he needed to take this asshole down.

Courtney tugged at his shirt and whispered his name.

Jack ignored her. "The people you just called family don't want anything to do with you, including your daughter."

Tom cocked his fist, and it landed smack in the middle of Jack's cheek. He jerked backward, smacking into Courtney, sending them both into the wall with a thud.

"Ugh," Courtney muttered.

Jack took her into his arms, kissing her temple. "Are you okay?"

Before she could answer, the sound of a camera shutter caught his attention.

"Nice to see the tables turned. Good to see you, Jack," the man with the camera said. "Got it all on film. Any comments, Tom?"

"No." Tom leaned closer to Jack and whispered, "Stay away from Courtney and Bri, or you'll find yourself in jail, again." Then Tom disappeared into the locker room.

"Jack? How about you? Would you like to make a statement about what just happened?"

"I'd rather focus on my game and forget about what Tom just did." Jack rubbed his jaw for good measure. "And it would be awesome if you could just let that picture die a quick death."

"I can do that."

"Thanks, man. See you on the course." He took Courtney by the hand and hightailed it outside.

"Thought you had to use the—"

"I'll use the one at the snack bar by the range."

"I can't believe he hit you," Courtney said as they approached a row of men standing at the range practicing their swing or having in-depth conversations with coaches and caddies. "Do you really think he'll keep that image to himself?"

"I think that depends on how the rest of the day goes," Jack admitted. But for now, he was going to have to push the entire ugly mess out of his mind.

He spent the next forty-five minutes warming up. He did his best to get into the zone, and no matter how many times he wanted to tell Courtney to zip it, he just continued to listen to her corrections and take them, knowing that she was right, even though he didn't want her to be.

"Jack," Courtney said with her hand on his biceps. "It's time."

Jack took in a deep breath. This was it. The beginning of his big comeback both into golf.

And life.

This was his chance to prove he wasn't washed-up, just yet.

With his head held up high, he strolled down the path and out to the first tee box.

Jack blinked as the sun hit his eyes. He adjusted his shades, hoping his hands didn't visibly shake. While the first tee time didn't generally catch a ton of spectators, with him coming back after years of being gone, it seemed a few people wanted to see if he still had what it took.

Of if he was going to lose his shit.

Again.

"Eight a.m. tee time. Jack Hollister and Mark Rundell," the announcer said.

The crowd cheered as he raised his hat and waved. Some shouted welcome back, and others told him to crawl in a hole and die. He shouldn't be surprised. Tom's dark side had never made its way into the real world. Somehow, that man managed to keep his drug use and cheating ways out of the limelight. Sure, the press all knew him to be a man who just couldn't settle down, even when he tried with the woman of his dreams, as he once called Courtney.

Jack gripped his club and squeezed. He wished he could understand why Courtney and her father didn't call Tom out on his bullshit, especially when a story would pop up, because they always did. But Tom always managed to make them go away or pivot the focus on all the wonderful things he did to give back to the community.

The same kind of bullshit Wendy and her father pulled, except when Jack fucked up, they tossed him under the bus.

"Jack," Courtney whispered. "Get out of your head and just play your game."

Jack stood still, waiting for Mark to hit the ball.

Mark couldn't have been more than twenty and from what Jack could gather, a damn good golfer.

Perhaps better than Jack had been at that age.

"Play the fairway to the right, hit a three wood," Courtney said after Mark had made a solid drive straight down the center.

"You've got to be kidding me. You want me to play conservative off the first tee when that pimply-faced kid just did that?"

"I want you to have a good showing and not embarrass yourself." She shoved the club in his face.

Jack took his three wood and swallowed. This was harder than he thought it was going to be. In the past, he could ignore the crowd and all their eyes collectively scrutinizing his every move. He took his practice swing, trying to ignore the few hecklers in the crowd.

Swish!

"Way to go, Jack," someone yelled.

"Nice shot," Mark said, tipping his hat. "For an old man."

"I'm just warming up," Jack said.

"You still hate it when I'm right." Courtney effortlessly lifted his bag and tossed it on her back.

He had to purse his lips to keep from grinning like a two-year-old playing in the mud. "I hate that you're carrying my bag. I'm a gentleman, and I didn't think this many people would show up for the early tee times." He shook his hands out. The last couple of practice rounds he had, this second shot had been his worst nightmare.

"You might not say gentlemanly words when you get my bill." She set his bag down and cupped her visor. "Green slopes to the right and to the back. It's subtle, until you get about ten yards from the pin. You hit it that far back, and you're going to roll right into that back sand trap. Stay short of the pin."

"You know he's going to go for it," Jack said.

"We don't give a shit what he does. He's young. Green. And greedy." Courtney handed him a seven iron. Back in the day, he would have used a six and choked down a little bit, taking a risk.

But today, he was going to do things Courtney's way.

"You're the boss." He hit the ball, and it landed about five yards past the pin and then rolled fifteen yards farther. "Shit. I hit it too hot."

"But you're not down the hill on the back side," Courtney said. "Easy two putt for par. Nice way to start the round."

The first few holes, the hecklers had started to get to him, but then Rudy and Bri showed up, following him from hole to hole. It gave him a sense of comfort to know they were there, even though they never once waved. Rudy did nod his head a few times, but little Bri acted like a golf professional.

By the time they got to the eighteenth hole, he was pleasantly surprised that he, not just Mark, still had a few followers left, especially since some of the bigger names had started to tee off.

"I'm glad you're back," Mark said, standing on the

eighteenth tee box. It was really the first time he spoke to Jack. "I used to love to watch you when I was a kid. I wanted to have your game, and dude, you've still got it."

"Thanks for making me feel old." Jack smiled at the young man.

"No problem." Mark smiled, turning his attention to his caddy.

"Nice buns," Courtney whispered.

"All the more reason you shouldn't be out here." He took the club she handed him, without question.

"Think boob," she said with a smile.

"You will never let me live that one down." Once he had caddied for her, and he asked how women hit the ball without their breasts getting in the way. She went about showing him exactly how, and it dawned on him that her breasts actually helped her swing.

"Nope, I never will."

He addressed the ball, and the second he started his backswing, he knew he should have stopped.

But he didn't.

And he hooked the ball to the trees on the far right of the fairway. "Fuck," he mumbled.

"It's okay." She hustled right next to him as he marched toward his ball.

Not a good way to end the day. It didn't matter that no one of importance was around; Jack needed this for his own confidence. He stood over his ball with his hands on his hips and studied the shot. He had a couple of choices, but all of them had some serious risks that could push this hole into a double bogey if he wasn't careful.

"Play the game. You can do this." She handed him a club.

He looked down at it. "You've got to be kidding." He sent her a glare. "You want me to pitch this short?"

She nodded. "The idea is to play smart. Now hit the goddamned ball." She stepped away from him.

He stepped back from the ball and looked through the trees. He looked down at his club, then glanced over at her. She didn't look back, but kept her focus on the green, with her hand over her visor.

"What the hell." He swung and the ball rolled about twenty yards short of the green. "Chip and putt for par. I can do that."

"I know you can." She patted his shoulder. "Let's finish this hole. Bri is getting antsy, and I want to get the hell out of here before we run into Tom again."

Jack rubbed his jaw. If Tom came at him a second time, Jack didn't think he'd be able to keep from retaliating.

He chipped the ball within five inches of the cup for an easy tap in. He shook Mark's hand before lifting Courtney in the air and giving her a good twirl. "Thank you," he said before kissing her temple. "I couldn't have done this without you."

"That's true," she said with a laugh.

Rudy greeted them at the roped-off area. Jack thought Rudy might actually have a smile on his face, instead of the look of doom he sported right now.

"Where's Bri?" Courtney asked with a bit of trepidation laced in her words.

"She's with a friend getting some pretzels for everyone," Rudy said. "We need to talk."

"That doesn't sound good." Jack followed Rudy to a table on the patio outside the clubhouse.

"I ran into Tom," Rudy started.

Jack held up his hand. "I don't know what he told you, but I didn't start it, and I didn't finish it. He's the one who hit me."

Rudy arched a brow.

"I don't think Tom told my dad about our little run-in with him," Courtney said. "And for the record, Dad, Jack is telling the truth. Tom tried to bait him, but Jack didn't bite."

"Well, that's good, but now we're going to need you to control that temper because Tom told me, and Bri—"

"He saw Bri?" Courtney asked with a high-pitched voice. She pressed her hands against the tabletop.

"It was a brief visit. He said hello, gave her a hug. There weren't any photographers around." Rudy patted her hand.

"That doesn't make me feel better," Courtney said, pushing her sunglasses up on her nose.

"Me neither," Jack said, chugging a glass of ice water. "Don't beat around the bush and get to the point." A few other golfers milled about. Some glanced in his direction, whispering; others just rolled their eyes.

He had a lot to prove.

"Bri might have told him that Jack was living with us."

Courtney gasped, covering her mouth. She caught Jack's gaze, holding him captive for a long moment.

He rubbed his lower lip with his thumb. "What else did Bri tell him?" The last thing any of them needed was drama with Tom. That would be a shitshow no one wanted to buy tickets for.

"That was it, but from the sideways glances the two of you are giving each other, I'd say something happened and Bri saw?" Rudy asked with a flat tone and an expressionless face. He'd always been a master at hiding his emotions, and that had driven Jack nuts as a rowdy teenager because you could never really tell what the man was thinking.

"Crap," Courtney mumbled. "She might have seen us kissing."

"Might have?" Rudy asked with a sarcastic laugh. "Well, she didn't tell him, or me, but she was certainly animated when talking about Jack."

"I'm sure he didn't like that, and if he plays bad, he's going to blame us somehow," Courtney said. "At least he won't be in town for too long."

"Only he mentioned regular visitation and told Bri she'd be seeing more of him," Rudy said. "And then he went on to tell me he was concerned about you and your decision-making and perhaps Bri might need to go stay with him."

Courtney slapped the table. "That bastard."

"Wait a second." Jack tugged his sunglasses off his face and set them on his thigh. "There is so much I don't understand about this situation, and I'm not going to ask for all the details right now, but what does you taking in a border have to do with custody and visitation?" He really wanted to ask more about Rudy's decision-making comment, but he'd leave that for later.

"Tom's threatened this since Courtney left," Rudy said. "It's all been bullshit just to hurt Courtney, but with you back, Tom's threats don't seem so idle anymore."

"Then I'll move out." No way would Jack let Courtney lose custody of her daughter.

Rudy's strong hand landed on his shoulder. "I'm going to let Courtney ultimately decide if we need to do that."

"I don't want either of you or especially Bri to be hurt by me being here. I can still work with you and live somewhere else," Jack said.

"I've been dealing with Tom for a while, and he's all talk. He doesn't really want Bri." Courtney shifted in her seat, crossing and recrossing her legs. "I really don't believe he'll come at me for custody, but I don't want him inserting himself into her life."

"I'll do whatever you want me to." Jack ran a hand through his hair. "I never wanted to hurt either of you or Bri by coming back here."

"Here comes Bri." Courtney stood. "I'm sure I'll be hearing from Tom soon enough. Until then, let's continue about our business as usual."

9

The following morning, Courtney tossed the newspaper on the kitchen table with a big huff. She leaned against the counter with her arms folded across her middle. “I don’t know why we thought Tom would quietly go away.”

“Unfortunately, if Jack hadn’t come back, we wouldn’t be having this conversation.”

“It’s not his fault that Tom’s a dick.”

“Look at you defending Jack.”

She shot her father a nasty look.

He shrugged. “Tom was like this before Jack came back into the picture. Now, do you want to tell me about this kiss that Bri witnessed? Because she’s like a bank vault. She wouldn’t tell me shit, and I tried every dirty trick in the book.”

Courtney couldn’t contain a slight proud smile. “I’m sure she said something.”

"Only that it wouldn't be polite for her to repeat a private moment like that."

"So, she told you, without telling you." Courtney laughed. "It wasn't a big deal, but not something I wanted Tom to hear, for a lot of reasons."

"Whether he truly believes it or not, I'm sure he thinks you and Jack are playing house under my roof and in front of Bri. And that is what we need to deal with." He picked up the newspaper and waved it in the air. "I hate to admit it, but I'm really happy they caught Tom hitting Jack. It really makes Tom look like an asshole, at least the way the newspaper spun it."

"This time." Courtney turned and pulled down a mug and lifted the coffee pot. "But you saw what Tom said about doing what he had to in order to protect his family and that the cameras didn't get the entire altercation."

"When he called to see if he could see Bri today, he brought up the accident." She looked at her father, shame crushing her heart. "He still has the text I sent him minutes before."

He took her hand in his strong protective one. "You were in a very dark place back then, but you're a different person now."

"And Tom will use what I did to take Bri from me."

Her father cupped her face. "I told you I would respect your wishes when it came to dealing with Tom only because I don't want Bri to be a pawn in his game to hurt us, but I'm seriously tired of watching you be afraid of him."

"He has more on me than I have on him, or at least that I can prove." Tears stung at the corners of her eyes.

Her father pulled her into his arms and cradled her head against his shoulder. "Honey, if Tom did try to use your suicide attempt—"

"Her what?" Jack's voice cut through her body like a sharp knife slicing into a perfectly cooked steak.

"You should tell him." Her father cupped her cheeks.

She nodded, taking in a deep cleansing breath.

"I'll go find Bri." Her father left the kitchen, leaving her to deal with Jack who looked as though someone had smacked him in the gut with his driver.

She knew that feeling.

"When? Why?" he asked as he closed the gap between them.

"About six months before I left Tom for good," she answered honestly. "We fought horribly and all the time. I would threaten to leave; he'd tell me to, and then he'd take Bri from me, and this particular time, he'd come at me with a laundry list of my transgressions and handed me a business card with his divorce lawyer's name on it. He told me that he'd already filed the paperwork, and I'd never see her again. He took Bri, and I didn't hear from either of them for two weeks."

"What did your father have to say about that?"

She swiped at her eyes. "My father didn't know what was going on until I tried to kill myself, though he suspected a lot of things, but since we didn't have a good relationship, there wasn't much he could do."

"What about the cops? Did you call them? Because that sounds like kidnapping to me."

"I didn't feel as though I could. My life had spiraled out of control and without Bri, I had nothing."

Jack drew his lips into a tight line. His nostrils flared, but he didn't say a word.

She cleared her throat. "Tom actually called the police on me, telling them I was a drug dealer, and they came into my house. Lucky for me, I'd already found the drugs and gotten rid of them. However, it proved to me that Tom would go to any length to keep me where he wanted, and I was just done."

Jack slammed his fist on the counter. "That man should be in prison."

She wasn't about to argue that point, but she needed to finish this story now or else she'd never be able to get through it. "I sent him a text message and told him what I was going to do and asked him if he had feelings for his daughter at all to let my father raise her."

Jack inhaled sharply, making a harsh gasping noise.

The sound rattled her courage and set her pulse on a wild ride. "Ten minutes after I sent that text, I drove his BMW into a tree at eighty miles an hour."

"Jesus Christ," Jack muttered, bringing his hand to his forehead. He rubbed his temples. "Is that how you got the concussion?"

"No. The story I tell people is that I tripped in the garage hitting my head on one of my golf clubs."

Jack arched a brow. "But that's not what happened." He lifted her chin.

"Nope. Tom thought I should know what it felt like when you hit him with your driver." She looked into his soft-green eyes and saw rage.

"Please tell me he never laid a hand on Bri."

She softened her expression. It was painfully obvious how much Jack loved her little girl. And how much Bri loved him.

It shouldn't hurt.

"No. He never hurt Bri physically. He has no connection with her other than his sperm, and even that he's questioned."

"He questioned her paternity?" He tugged at his shirt. "Let's go outside." He pushed open the door and guided her down the path toward the tire swing. "Get in." He pointed to the swing.

Moments passed as he pushed her gently, and she pumped her legs. The sun moved toward the center of the sky. A few clouds danced with the slight northerly breeze picking up flowery spring scents.

"Tell me what happened with you and Tom." He stopped the tire and sat down in front of her, fiddling with her sandals.

"Okay, but you have to tell me something." She cocked her head. "And you have to let me take you shopping."

"Shopping?" Both eyebrows arched.

She nodded. "And I get to pick the clothes and pay the bill."

"Nah-ah, no way." He held up his hand.

"Then I'll shop without you, but you really need some more clothes. Two shirts aren't cutting it. And we both know the bank book is nonexistent." She jumped down from the swing. "Ugh." Her foot caught on a root, and she tumbled forward.

"Umph." Jack didn't have enough time to react.

She landed on top of him. "Ouch."

He chuckled as he wrapped his arms around her, his strong hands pressing against her spine.

She froze. His gaze captured hers and couldn't break free from its grip. She saw compassion. She saw her friend. But she saw something else and felt the electricity between them. That feeling had to be shut down. "Crap. Sorry." She wiggled free of his grip and rolled to the side. "So." She brushed the dirt from her face. "We have a deal."

"I won't let you buy my clothes." He scowled.

"Be humble, Jack. You can't go on tour with two shirts. You can pay me back when you start placing. Besides, I'll use Tom's money. That should make it worthwhile for you."

"That money should be for Bri."

She sighed. "How much money do you have left?" She yanked at his arm. She stumbled backward as he shrugged his arm free of her grip.

"I don't need your charity or your pity."

"This is neither, and you know it."

He tossed his hands wide. "Fine, but the first check I get I'm giving all of it to you and your father."

"Of course, you are," she said with a smile.

He leaned against the big tree. "You said you'd tell me about your marriage."

"Then you have to tell me something." She couldn't believe that she was going to tell him the ugly truth.

And then ask for his honesty in return.

But they'd come this far, it was time to heal old wounds.

"Deal. I want to know why you let Tom play these games with you and Bri."

She backed up against the counter. "Because he has the right. I can't deny him. In the custody agreement, he technically gets her once a month and every other holiday, but it has to be set up with me ahead of time. The way the law works, if he doesn't visit her at all, I can nail his ass for abandonment and my transgressions might not mean anything."

His strong hand brushed against the side of her face. "So, you plan on taking him to court?"

"Eventually, when enough time has gone by. He hasn't paid child support in the last few months, and I stopped reminding him. I know it's a sucky game, but I don't know what else to do."

His breath felt warm on her face. He cupped the back of her head, tilting it. His mouth brushed over hers like a feather floating in the wind. She couldn't deny herself the simple pleasure of the way his full lips felt against hers. The way his body drew her near, giving her the strength, she lacked.

She felt safe in his arms.

"What's going on with us?" he asked.

"Stuff that shouldn't be happening," she said.

"What if I want more of what that kiss promised?"

Her heart fluttered so fast it was difficult to breathe. "I can't, Jack. Not now. We're both still picking up the pieces of our lives. The timing couldn't be worse."

"I can respect that," he said.

She smiled at him. "My turn."

He threw his arms wide and laughed. "What do you want to know?"

Might as well go for the jugular. "Did you sleep with Wendy the night of my father's birthday party?" she asked. Wendy had rubbed it in her face, but they never looked like a couple until he announced they were getting married. Before that, Wendy would hang on him, rubbing her breasts against him, and flirt with him shamelessly. However, Jack never seemed overly interested in her, other than what her father had to offer him, and maybe the drugs she provided.

"What the fuck kind of question is that?"

"We had a deal, remember?"

"Oh, for Pete's sake. No. I didn't sleep with her that night."

"When did you then?"

"Excuse me?" he asked with wide eyes.

"When did you first take Wendy to bed?"

"Again, why the fuck do you want to know that?" His gaze caught hers with a mixture of grief and sorrow. "Why does it matter?"

"It matters to me. She threw it in my face, on more than one occasion."

"Okay, wait a second." He rubbed his forehead. "Let's back this up a second. When did she tell you I first slept with her?"

"For months before you married her. I made the mistake of telling her I had a crush on you, and she, in turn, shit on me by telling me you and she were hot and heavy under the sheets. She even went as far as to describe a few things for me."

Jack laughed, but it wasn't a funny kind of laugh, more like painful choking on one's own curses. "I'm sorry she did that. She used our relationship to her advantage in more ways than one."

"Of course, she did."

"When I first started talking to James, she'd tell me what a crush you had on me. Told me it bordered on obsession and I should be careful."

"You should be careful? Of me?" Courtney asked. "That's ridiculous."

"I know. But she also pointed out your age and that if one person even thought something was happening with us, it could cause me a lot of problems. I know we've always been close, but at the time you were only seventeen."

"All true, but that still doesn't answer my question."

"I slept with her only once before I married her. And that was two months after your father's birthday. I had a little too much to drink and didn't have a condom."

"You've got to be kidding me," she mumbled. "Jesus. Once out of the gate and she's knocked up. Same thing with me and Tom."

He laughed. "Only with us, there was never a baby."

"Shit, Jack, I'm so sorry."

He jumped to his feet and held out his hand. "So was I. Now let's get this shopping shit over with."

10

The following morning, Jack sat on the edge of his bed and toyed with one of his new golf shirts and contemplated his past and his present, but he wasn't sure what his future would hold. In less than twenty-four hours, he'd be on an airplane to his next tournament with Courtney by his side.

Dreams about the night Courtney had told him she loved him and subsequently kissed him had haunted him for years. It was a kiss like no kiss he'd ever had before. And it amazed him he could remember it so vividly. He touched his lips.

But Wendy had told him she was pregnant. He had to do right by his baby. Too bad Wendy had never really been pregnant. Her way to make sure he walked away from Courtney.

A moment he will always regret almost as much as having to take Courtney's money. He needed to win a tournament. Even a small one. He wanted to pay her back.

He pulled one of his new shirts over his head, tucking it into his pants. Rudy wanted him practicing every morning by sunrise. Nothing new there.

Quietly, he made his way down the stairs and out to the range.

"Good morning." Rudy smiled, dumping a bucket of balls on the mat. "I have a job for you."

"Huh?" Jack stopped in the middle of his swing.

"A job, ya know one that pays," Rudy said playfully.

"I don't want your money." Jack leaned against his club.

"That's why I found you a job."

"I don't understand." Jack rubbed his clean-shaven face.

"I know how hard this has been for you. I want you to be happy, and golf makes you happy. But you need money to do that."

"I'm sorry, Rudy. I didn't think about what your situation… Courtney's situation would be like."

"Money's not an issue. But your pride is. I can tell by the way you have been hitting the ball." He narrowed his eyes.

"What's the job?"

"Helping out in the kids' program and giving private lessons at the club."

"Excuse me? Me teach?" Jack's eyes flew from their sockets. He had to blink to bring them back in. "I can't teach."

"Yes, you can. I think you taught Courtney more about golf than I did."

"What about the schedule? I'll be in and out a lot."

"I'll make your schedule, since I know when you'll be gone. Also, we're gonna start training a new caddie."

Jack stopped his stretching and glared at Rudy. "I want Courtney."

"For a while, but she needs to be here with Bri. I can't have her gone every weekend."

Jack took in a deep breath and started swinging. Rudy was right. But he didn't like it. "Larry?"

"Hopefully."

Jack nodded.

"It might take a while, but I suspect once he's finished with Burke, he'll sign on with us. I want you and Courtney to start playing a round or two a week. Maybe more if I've got a caddy for her to look at until we can get Larry."

Rudy placed a ball on the mat.

Jack swung. "Ahhh, shit."

Rudy took Jack by the shoulders. "I'm proud of you, son. You came up from a dark place. I don't know what happened. Honestly, I don't care. I'm just glad your back. Neither Courtney nor I will turn our backs on you. But you have to pull it together under pressure or your career will be null and void." Rudy gave him a good shake.

His insides continued to tremble as if he were coming off a three-day binge. "I spent the last two years trying to figure out how to come back."

"Here? Or golf?" Rudy moved Jack's club with him. "End the backswing here," he added then stepped back.

"It's not just about golf. I want my life back." Jack addressed the ball, but it didn't feel right. He swayed left and right before steadying his body and refocusing on the ball. "Before I let Wendy and her father ruin it."

Rudy gave him a fatherly glare.

"Okay, I ruined my life the day I married that woman."

"So, let's not go making any more mistakes like that one. No women when you're on the road."

Jack stepped up to the ball. "Not sure I'd know what to do with one."

Rudy laughed. "Keep it that way."

The practice went uphill from that point. Jack was finally starting to relax. He hit for another half hour, then Rudy called it quitting time.

Rudy slung his arm over Jack's shoulders as they walked toward the house. "You and Courtney are gonna play this morning. Then I want you to help her with the kids' program."

Jack swallowed. "Christ, Rudy. I know I agreed to do things your way."

"My way means you do what I say in every aspect of your life."

Jack stopped and turned to face his mentor. "What the hell do I know about teaching? And kids?"

A slow smile drew on Rudy's face. "First, you're really good with Bri. These kids are no different.

Second, this is more about you than them. Trust me." Rudy left Jack standing in the walkway.

"Trust you," Jack muttered, shaking his head. Bri was unique. And easy to be around. But a whole group of kids? And teach them the game? Jack didn't think he could do it.

He didn't think he wanted to.

"Would you lighten up?" Courtney gave her bag to one of the bag boys.

"Easy for you to say," Jack said under his breath.

"Come on, Jack. They're just kids. They don't bite. At least none that I'm aware of." She couldn't believe how uncomfortable he was dealing with a group of pint-size adults.

"Hi, Courtney!" A bubbly little boy skipped down the cart path.

"Hi, Steven." Courtney waved to the boy and his mom.

"Can I hang with all the moms?" Jack whispered. "She's cute."

"She's married." Courtney couldn't help the surge of jealousy that passed through her system, making her cheeks heat. The young woman that Jack currently stared at was a beautiful, lonely trophy wife who she suspected banged every young man she could get her hands on.

"It was a joke," Jack said.

A few more children came running along the parking lot, as did one of Courtney's least favorite mothers...well, stepmother.

"Hello, Andrew. How are you?" She patted the young boy's head. He couldn't help who his father remarried.

"I'm good. Who's that?" He pointed to Jack.

"The name is Jack, and I'm helping out Courtney today."

"Cool." Andrew raced over to where all the other children had gathered.

"Jack Hollister?" Mrs. Wellington took her big black designer shades off and stuck them between her big fake boobs. "Is that really you?"

Jack pushed his sunglass on the top of his head. "Oh, hello, Lucy. How are you?"

Courtney knew that the beautiful and slutty Mrs. Lucy Wellington knew Jack. She'd been going after golfers for years but decided that older rich men were more stable, had more money, and were easier to cheat on with the pool boy.

"Mrs. Rivers—" Lucy started.

Courtney adjusted her visor. "It's Wade, but I'd prefer if you called me Courtney."

"Of course," Lucy said as she curled her fingers around Jack's biceps. "How long has it been?"

"Years," Jack said.

"What brings you back?" Lucy asked. She ran her perfectly manicured fingers up and down his arm as if he were a kitten needing to be brushed.

Courtney wanted to roll her eyes. It had been all over the news that Jack Hollister was making a comeback.

"I thought it was high time I take Tom Rivers down a few pegs."

"Last time you tried to do that didn't you land yourself in jail?" Lucy dropped her hands to the sides.

"So, married with kids, huh? That's a twist."

"You sound so surprised." She folded her arms and tapped her stupid high heels.

"Considering the last time I saw you, I sure am." Jack plopped his glasses back to his nose. "Of course, I'm sure he's a real gem. And I mean that in the sense that he can keep you covered in them." Jack tipped his hat and strolled toward the putting green and the children.

Courtney swallowed. If she spoke like that to any of the members, her father would have her hide.

"Looks like he hasn't changed." Lucy pushed her left hip out. "You better teach him to behave. or the membership is going to have all of you fired."

"I apologize for Jack, and I'll speak to him."

"You do that, or I'll be having my husband bring it up to the board."

Courtney smoothed out her pants, took a deep breath, and headed for Jack and the kids.

"Okay, kiddos," she said. "Let's start with practicing some putting. Hillary, will you please work with them for a few minutes. I need a word with Jack."

"Sure thing," Hillary, one of the assistant pros, said.

"I get the feeling that I'm about to be lectured." Jack stuffed his hands in his pockets.

"Damn right you are," Courtney said. "What the hell was that about?"

"That chick's bad news."

"Mrs. Wellington—"

"Cut the formalities," Jack said. "Lucy has always been a gold digger with a cocaine habit."

Courtney gasped. She'd heard a lot of stories about a lot of different members, but she tried to ignore them, especially when they had a connection to her past life. She'd seen Lucy back in the day hanging with Tom, Wendy, Jack, and the rest of the gang, but Lucy seemed to be more on the peripheral edges of the group.

"It doesn't matter what she was or what you think of her now," Courtney said. "Her husband is one of the most powerful members on this golf course. She's not the woman you want to go pissing off."

"I'll work on my delivery next time, but if she touches my body again, all bets are off," he said. "Are we done?"

"What is your problem?" Courtney asked.

"Nothing. I think we have kids waiting for us."

Courtney peeked her head in her daughter's room. It physically hurt her heart that she was going to have to be away from her little girl for a few nights. She smiled at her sleeping Bri. Everything Courtney had been through had been worth it because of Bri.

She heard the door close in the kitchen.

Jack. She needed to get this over with. It would fester and drive her wacko if she didn't. So she headed for the kitchen.

Jack stood in front of the microwave with his hands on his hips. She shook her head. His backside made her want to rush over there and squeeze the Charmin. "You shouldn't stand so close. That thing is really old."

"Yes, mother." He smiled over his shoulder and shifted to the left. "Want some popcorn?"

The popcorn bounced about inside its bag as the smell filled the kitchen. Her insides jumped about in the same manner. She could feel her pulse buck and pop. She shook her hands out. "I'd like to talk to you if you don't mind." She pulled out a bowl and two wine glasses, then poured some of her favorite white.

"Sounds serious. Can I pass? I just got my ass chewed out by your father." He poured the popcorn in the bowl.

"You deserved it."

"I'm well aware," he said flatty. "Shall we take this little party outside?"

She glanced toward the door.

"Come on." He picked up the bowl and one of the glasses. He breezed by her without looking.

"You're in a mood." She grabbed her glass and followed. His mood meant this conversation could go south real quick, but perhaps that would be for the best. She needed to deal with Tom so that she and Bri could have their lives back without constantly worrying that Tom would swoop in and destroy it.

The night sky lit up like the Fourth of July with all the stars. The moon was almost full, and a warm breeze did nothing to keep her insides from burning.

"I feel like I'm seventeen again," she admitted once they settled against the tree that held the tire swing. A spot where they had shared many nights talking together in the past.

"Why is that?" He tossed some popcorn in his mouth.

"While I'm not going to profess something totally outrageous like I did that night, I do find myself with all those same feelings."

"So do I," he said, sipping his wine.

"What exactly does that mean?" She felt a jab to her heart.

He gave her a pointed look. "It means we, my dear, are in the same predicament."

"I doubt that."

"Really? Let's test that theory." He leaned closer to her and cupped her chin.

Her pulse quickened, and her gaze diverted to his lips at the precise moment he licked them.

She licked her own in anticipation. He pulled away. "Like I said, same damn predicament." He turned his gaze toward the sky.

"You're attracted to me?" she asked, even though she

knew the answer, her insecurities reared their ugly heads.

"Ya think?" came his sarcastic response.

She tossed a kernel of popcorn at him.

"Sorry. I've always hated it when you put yourself down. You're a beautiful woman. How can you not know I'm attracted to you?"

"Okay, so maybe I get that today, but you never told me you thought I was pretty or that you saw me that way back then."

"Did too." He tapped his index finger against the center of his chest.

"You so did not," she said. "I think your exact words were that I was growing into a beautiful woman but wasn't quite there yet and needed to find a 'boy' my own age."

"Same thing." He shrugged.

"I want us to be friends. But nothing more. I can't. Not now and maybe never."

"Why?"

She rubbed her sweaty palms on her pants. "There are lots of reasons. But mostly because right now I have to concentrate on getting Tom out of mine and Bri's life for good."

"I can respect that."

"Friends?"

"Always." He took her hand and held it. "I never meant to hurt you. I was scared and confused, and Wendy lied to me."

"She lied to everyone." Courtney desperately

wanted to yank her hand from his.

He shook his head. "She told me she miscarried two days after we married."

"Jack, I'm sorry." Courtney touched his cheek, then pulled back. "My timing couldn't have come at a worse time that day."

"I wish it came about two hours earlier," he muttered.

She blinked. "It wouldn't have changed anything. You didn't feel the same way about me. And you would've still married her." She looked down at the bowl of popcorn. "And I never really felt that way. It was a crush."

"Oh, my God. Stop backpedaling. You cared for me back then, and you still care just as much for me now."

She scowled. "You just said you understood."

"You're killing me." He tossed back half his wine. "I understand that getting involved with anyone, me included, while dealing with this Tom shit isn't a good idea right now. And I'm going to be out on the road a lot with golf. Not an ideal way to start a dating relationship, but I'm learning to be a patient man when I want something."

"Patience isn't a strong suit for either of us, and even when I've gotten Tom out of our lives, I will need to move out of this house and into a place on my own." She held up her hand. "All on my own."

"You told me you were in love with me that night, and if we're being honest here, I already knew that before you told me." He pressed his finger against her lips. "And now here's a really heavy dose of reality for you. I'm pretty sure I was in love with you too."

"I was a teenager. That's ridiculous."

"Is it?"

"You loved me then, and you feel something for me now," he said. "And I want to explore what I feel for you."

"I find you hot and wouldn't mind a roll in the hay," she said. "But that would just be wild animal sex, and it would destroy our friendship. I've missed you too much to risk losing you again."

He polished off his glass and leaned closer. "I don't want to have sex with you. I want to make love with you."

She swallowed her breath. "How much have you had to drink tonight?"

"You don't believe me?"

"We both want mutually satisfying sex, but we can't have it with each other. I bet Lucy would be willing." Shit. She cringed. She really didn't want to pick a fight. She only wanted to admit she was attracted to him, but that in the end she only wanted his friendship, nothing more.

"I don't want Lucy. I want you." He stood. "And I don't want you one time, or a couple of times. I want to be with you in a relationship that has the potential to become permanent, and I'm willing to wait for it." He turned on his heels and headed into the house, leaving her sitting under the tree wondering what the hell had just happened.

11

"Are you going to ignore me for the next four days?" Jack pulled the rental car into the hotel parking lot.

"And I thought it was you ignoring me." She stared out the window.

"We need to talk about my confession." He waved his hand in front of her face.

"I think we need to stop doing that."

He laughed, although he didn't find it funny, but for now he'd let it go. "This hotel is too expensive."

"We got a good deal," Courtney said. "And for my room, I used points."

"I hate that you did that." He took the key cards and headed toward the elevators and their adjoining rooms. "You're my caddy; I should be paying you."

That posed a different problem, but he was going to do his best to keep his eye on the prize.

And not the woman of his dreams.

"You'll pay me back when you start winning," she said. "I'm going to call home, and then we can go to the restaurant across the street for dinner."

"I'll leave the door open in between rooms. Just open yours and let me know when you're ready." Jack made a beeline for the bathroom to splash cold water on his face. Being this close to Courtney all night was going to be a challenge. He flopped onto the bed, stretching his arms wide, and stared at the ceiling fan.

A tap at the door startled him.

"Bri wants to talk to you." Courtney stood between the two rooms holding out her phone.

"Is she okay?" Jack propped himself up on his elbows.

"She wants to wish you good luck."

Jack took the phone. "Hey there, munchkin."

"Hi, Jack. Grandpa is pacing outside."

Jack laughed. "I'm sure he is, but you tell him that I'm going to get a bite to eat and go right to bed. And tomorrow I plan on crushing it."

"I'm going to watch on TV!"

He doubted he'd get much screen time, but as long as he made the cut, he'd be happy. "When they announce my name at the first tee box, I'll blow you a kiss."

"I'll blow one right back," Bri said with a giggle.

"Here's your mom. Be a good girl for your grandpa."

"I will. I love you, Jack."

He sucked in a deep breath. His heart squeezed tight and struggled to beat normally. Hearing those words fall so genuinely from the little girl's lips drew tears to his eyes. He knew she meant that. Her innocence wouldn't allow that kind of betrayal.

But he wasn't worthy of her love.

"I love you right back," he said before handing the phone to Courtney. He closed his eyes and breathed in slowly, as if he were just chilling, waiting for his caddy to finish her phone call.

Only he was dying a little bit inside.

Everything he wanted in life he'd found, only they didn't belong to him.

He felt the bed shift. He opened his eyes to find Courtney leaning against the headboard, hugging one of the pillows with a deep expression.

"What's wrong?" he asked.

"Nothing."

"You're furrowing your brow, and whenever you do that, something is troubling you."

She chuckled. "I suppose I do."

He scooted to a sitting position and tapped her temple with his index finger. "So, what's going on in that pretty little head of yours?"

"She's falling in love with you, and it's going to break her little heart when you walk out of her life."

"What makes you think I'm going to walk away?" He never planned on disappearing again. He wanted Rudy, Courtney, and Bri to be a part of his life. The problem was he wanted Courtney in a forever way, and if he couldn't have that, he wasn't sure how healthy it would be for all of them if he were to stick around so closely.

That said, he'd make sure he would protect Bri's heart. That was a promise he knew he could keep.

"You've got the most natural talent of anyone I've ever met."

"You don't get out enough then."

She laughed. "Seriously though. If you can keep your head out of your ass and stay away from women and drugs, you'll be at the top of the money charts by the end of the year and making a sweep of the majors soon enough."

"Thanks for the confidence, but that doesn't mean I'll be abandoning you or Bri." He arched a brow. "I'm not Tom."

"No. You're definitely not him. But in some ways, you're worse."

"What the fuck does that mean?" He bolted upright and stared at her with his mouth gaping open.

"Bri's a smart girl. She knows the difference between when someone genuinely cares about her and her family and when someone is just going through the motions. But Tom is her father, and he's supposed to love and protect her."

"But he doesn't. And I'm not following."

"If you'd be quiet and let me finish, I'll explain it to you." She cocked her head with a sarcastic grin.

"Go ahead." He waved his hand.

"It took Tom four months before he held her when no one was looking. It drove me nuts what a great show he'd put on for the cameras, and oh boy, it did a number on Bri."

Jack would never completely understand why Courtney let Tom do that to Bri, or to her, but he'd never judge her for it. "Bri is bouncing back nicely from all the crap her father has put her through."

"I'm responsible for some of that," Courtney said. "What you have to understand is that Bri doesn't tell her father that she loves him. Not that she sees or talks to him often. But when you leave her life, it's going to break her little heart."

"I'm not leaving. I'll be on the road a lot, but I keep telling you that I'm a patient man and I'll wait."

"You don't get it," she said under her breath. "If you and I were to happen, Tom would insert himself into our lives and into Bri's. I can't have that."

"Courtney." Jack reached out and lifted her chin. "I'm here, and he's barely inserted himself back into your life. He's all talk."

"You don't know that."

"He can't hurt you anymore."

"He's got that text that proves I tried to kill myself. He has pictures of me doing drugs after Bri was born. He has a plethora of shit on me, and he'll take Bri from me. When we got divorced, the deal was I got Bri, and neither one of us aired our dirty laundry."

Jack shifted on the bed and leaned against the headboard. "What if there was some dirty laundry on him that had nothing to do with you?"

"What does that mean?" she asked with wide eyes.

"I lived through some dark days when I was deep into my drug use, and some really bad shit went down. There is this one night that is very fuzzy, but Tom was there, and something happened. There was talk that Tom could have been responsible. However, it went away."

"What happened?" Courtney jumped to her knees.

"I was wasted, and the details are beyond fuzzy."

"You're talking about the night Taylee was raped?"

Jack swallowed. That had been a horribly fucked-up night. Someone had slipped something into Taylee's drink, and she woke up in the backyard naked, beaten, and without a clue as to who hurt her. The only memory she had was of doing lines of cocaine with Jack.

"I know you didn't rape her," Courtney said.

Jack let out a sarcastic chuckle. "That was proven without doubt." But it had been the straw that broke the camel's back, sending Jack into oblivion. A month after that party, he'd had words on the driving range with Tom. Jack had been higher than a kite that morning. His sham of a marriage was over. The press had a field day with the whispers of rape and his womanizing ways, which he couldn't deny. He'd gotten caught with his pants down more than once, and on that morning as well. His sponsors were pulling away left and right. He knew he was washed-up and his career was over. He'd been out of his mind, and he couldn't even remember what he'd been thinking, other than he'd been hoping he'd win the tournament, get a hefty check, and then maybe go to Aruba.

"But someone at that party did." Fuck. Deep down he'd always believed he'd known who'd done it. Hell, he and Taylee had talked about who could have, and one name kept coming up.

Tom.

Courtney hugged the pillow tighter. "You think it was Tom."

"I honestly don't know." That wasn't a lie.

"Taylee hasn't spoken to me since that night, and about a year ago she moved to San Diego." Courtney banged her head against the headboard. "Tom has a violent streak. I wouldn't put it past him."

"Did he ever…did he…" Jack couldn't bring himself to trip over the words rape when it came to Courtney.

She didn't have to say anything. The pain etched in her pale-blue eyes said it all.

"Jesus, Courtney."

"We had a volatile relationship."

Jack wiggled his fingers. He wanted to put his fist through the wall. "Volatile? That fucking asshole should be in jail."

"I know. And if I could put him there, I would. But the best I have is getting him legally out of mine and Bri's life. I spoke to my lawyer, and we're so close to getting him on abandonment. All I want is to have a little more control where even if he does come at me with my past drug use or my suicide attempt, it won't matter."

"I'm so sorry I've let you down," Jack said. "I don't ever want to be that person again. I care so much for you."

He yanked her into his arms and buried his face in the warmth of her neck, feeling her pulse beat wildly against his skin.

Her soft hands splayed across his back and moved slowly toward his shoulders before she gripped him so tightly he thought he might suffocate. She tucked her face into his chest. "Jack?"

"Yes, babe." He cupped the back of her head, stroking her hair.

Her body stilled as she took in a deep breath and lifted her head. "My father has a rule about these things," she mumbled before she leaned into him, pressing her mouth over his. Her warm lips gently stroked his, sending a shock wave throughout his entire system.

He wrapped his arms around her firm, thin frame and pulled her against his hard body as he rolled to his side.

Her tongue dance with his to the sweet music their soft moans created. Her hands clasped around his neck, she planted tiny wet kisses across his face until she landed on his mouth once again. She tasted like honey and felt like warm sunshine in his arms.

She felt like home.

"I've been told I'm a rule breaker." He nibbled on her earlobe, dotting her sweet neck with kisses, making his way down toward her soft mounds pressing against her blouse.

Her fingers dug into his scalp as he fiddled with the buttons, exposing a lacy tan bra with a front clasp. He knew he should take his time and not act like a horny teenager, but staring at her wide-open shirt and her hard nipples pushing against the fabric of her undergarment, there was no way he was going to wait to see the beauty that lay beneath.

The moment he exposed her breasts to the cool air-conditioning, her nipples tightened and puckered. He reached out and traced the outline of her areola with his index finger.

She gasped, sucking in a breath. Goosebumps spread over her milky soft skin.

He drew a nipple into his mouth and sucked hard, twisting and swirling it.

"Oh, Jack," she said as she arched her back. Her fingers dug into his shoulders, and she wrapped her legs around his body, pulling him down on hers. She rolled her hips against his hardness, driving him over the edge.

He stood, grabbing her from behind the knees and yanking her to the foot of the bed. As quickly as he could, he removed the rest of her clothing. Staring at her naked body, the oxygen left his lungs as if an elephant had sat on his chest and wasn't getting up anytime soon.

Dropping to his knees, he lifted her legs and rested them over his shoulders. He kissed the back side of her calves and licked his way up her inner thighs. "You're so beautiful." He lifted his gaze and once again, she stole his breath.

She'd propped herself up on her elbows and stared down at him with laden eyes and a sexy smile.

His heart nearly stopped. It had been months since he'd had sex, and all of a sudden, he wasn't sure he knew what he was doing, much less had the ability to satisfy a woman. He swallowed. Hard.

She licked her lips as she raised her hand and brought it to her breasts.

"You're going to be the death of me," he whispered as he lowered his head and slowly dragged his tongue across her, tasting what could only be described as the sweetest most decadent thing he's ever had the pleasure of tasting.

He got drunk on her, and he knew without a doubt there'd never be another woman who could affect him the way Courtney did. He suspected that back then.

He knew it now.

She tightened around his fingers and tongue. Her heels slammed into his back as she arched, crying out his name.

It wasn't until she pulled at his hair that he decided he should stop.

He lifted his head and smiled.

She stared at him with wide eyes. Her chest heaved up and down as if she'd gotten the wind knocked out of her.

Gently, he reached between her legs and touched her tight nub.

Her body jerked and quivered.

She dropped her head back. "Oh, dear Lord," she whispered, biting down on her lower lip. "Please. I want to feel you inside me."

He stood. "Your wish is my command."

"And you should be careful standing like that."

Before he had a chance to catch his breath, she was on her knees with her hands pushing his jeans over his hips. "What are you doing?"

She curled her fingers around the length of him."What you would wish for if you had the chance to ask for it."

He groaned while her hot tongue flicked out of her mouth and rolled over the tip. Her hands glided gently, but firmly up and down his shaft. "I'm not complaining," he managed with a ragged breath. "But I didn't wish for that...out loud."

She held him in her hands and looked up at him, licking her lips with a wicked smile. "But you did wish for it inside your head."

"Oh, hell yes." He ripped his shirt off and tossed it to the floor. His heart pounded so fast he thought it might jump right out of his chest. He'd dreamed about this moment for a long time, and he knew it would blow his mind, but never in a million years did he believe it would bring him to his knees, reducing him to near tears.

He kicked his jeans off and pushed Courtney onto

her back and lowered herself between her legs. Slowly, he entered her, watching as her eyelids fluttered.

She rolled her hips, encouraging him to pick up the pace, and while he wanted to do everything in his power to make it last. He wouldn't deny her what she wanted.

Her heels dug into his ass. "Oh, my God, Jack." She gripped his shoulders with her fingers so hard he thought she might have drawn blood. Her body trembled, pulling him into her orgasm. His climax spilled out, making him shudder. He couldn't catch his breath. His lungs burned.

His heart ached.

He loved this woman.

Loved her more than life itself.

He loved her more than golf.

And he knew what he had to do, even if it meant he'd once again lose everything to do it.

12

"Dad, it was fantastic." Courtney raised her glass of wine and took a sip. The entire weekend had been beyond anything she could have imagined.

And it wasn't just the great sex.

Though she'd like to believe that it helped how Jack played the game. Of course, if he hadn't won, or placed, she'd have to blame it on the extracurricular activities.

"I've never seen him so focused before. I know it's only the second tournament, but I do believe he's changed."

"So do I." Her father raised his glass. "But I worry about the mounting pressure not to mention what money does to that young man. Jack's always had an eye for quality, and he likes having the best."

She understood her father's concern. She'd be lying to herself if the same thought didn't rattle around in the back of her mind. "Only, he's seen the other side of what fame and fortune can do to a person. Did you see his interviews? That humbleness wasn't a game. He wasn't playing to what he thinks everyone wants to hear. That's the real Jack. The one we both love."

"Love?" Her father lowered his voice and raised a brow.

She rolled her eyes.

"I did notice you've been glowing ever since you got back."

Heat rose to her cheeks. Butterflies filled her gut. "I'm happy for Jack."

"I know, but something else has changed. Or happened and based on those big wide eyes of yours, I'm not sure I want to know."

One of the conditions of her moving home when she left Tom had been she had to be honest, something she hadn't been with her father since she'd turned eighteen. Well, she was now twenty-four and other than the constant problems Tom brought to her world, she'd successfully turned her life around. She even planned on moving out, but her father begged her to stay. He liked having his granddaughter around, and since he was single and had no prospects, Courtney couldn't leave him.

And why would she.

The house was huge, and they got along great.

She opened her mouth to deny her father's spot-on observation, but all that came out was a noise that reminded her of a billy goat.

"Oh hell," she muttered.

"You broke my rules," he said with a stern voice, but the right side of his mouth twitched.

"You have rules for caddies? Because last time I checked, as a caddie, I work for Jack, not you."

Her father waved his finger under her nose. "Oh no, you don't, young lady."

"Don't you young lady me." She sat up a little taller. "I am a grown woman with a kid of my own."

"This is true." Her father let out a long breath, leaning back on the sofa. He lifted his feet and rested them on the counter. "So, you and Jack, huh?"

"I don't know," she admitted. "Since we got home, things got weird. And there's the issue of Tom."

"I think I know why Jack's being weird."

"What do you mean?" She set her glass on the end table and tucked her feet under her butt. She glanced toward the stairs. Bri had begged for Jack to put her to bed, and he'd been more than willing. That meant it would take twice as long because that little girl had him wrapped around her pinky.

"He saw the check that came in the mail from Tom."

"I would have told him." Courtney let out an exasperated sigh. "The lawyer said that while money doesn't make up for his lack of visitation, it's enough to keep him in the picture."

"And we all know he paid that money because of Jack."

She pinched the bridge of her nose. "That's going to screw with his game."

"What about his heart? And yours?"

She snapped her gaze toward her father. "His game is all we need to concern ourselves with. That's why he came back."

"That's not the only reason he came back, and if I know him as well as I think I do, golf is actually at the bottom of his list." Her father's feet hit the floor with a heavy thud. He leaned forward and cupped her cheeks. "You both deserve to be happy. Don't let Tom stand in your way." He kissed her forehead and headed toward the stairs.

She wished life were that simple. Being with Jack was easy, and she loved him, no doubt in her mind.

Or her heart.

She didn't think he loved her back, but she knew he cared deeply, and love took time to develop. She'd had years of loving him, and he'd had years of fighting himself. What they needed was time and space from the insanity their youth and past had created.

Only, Tom would make that impossible.

Jack leaned against the doorjamb and stared at Bri. Her pudgy little fingers curled around the stuffed puppy he'd given her earlier. She'd fallen asleep halfway through the third time he'd read *Three Billy Goats Gruff.*

His cell buzzed in his back pocket.

Taylee: How'd you find me?

Jack: I ran into your mother.

He wasn't about to tell her that he'd run into her mother about a year ago.

Taylee: I'll have to remind her that I want nothing to do with anyone in golf.

Jack: I appreciate you getting back to me. Can we talk?

Taylee: That's what we're doing.

Jack let out a slight chuckle.

Jack: About Tom.

Taylee: No. I've put that entire ordeal behind me.

Jack: I hate to ask and wouldn't if Courtney and her daughter weren't involved and Tom wasn't screwing with them.

Taylee: Screwing with them how? And why does this involve me?

Jack: Can we just talk on the phone?

Taylee: I can't right now. Tomorrow morning. Call me at 9.

He stuffed his phone back into his pocket. That would have to do.

"Hey, you," Courtney whispered as she rubbed her soft hands across his shoulders. "She's so proud of you."

He pointed to his trophy. "I hope you don't mind; I gave it to her."

"Not at all," Courtney said. "How does it feel to win again?"

"I won't lie, it feels damn fantastic." He laced his fingers through hers and tugged her toward his room. "But it's bittersweet."

"Why?"

"Because I know the competition and most of the big names weren't there."

She stopped dead in her tracks, yanking her hand away. "Do not belittle that win," she said a little too loudly.

He brought his index finger to his lips and waved her down the hallway.

Reluctantly she followed.

After stepping into his bedroom, he closed the door. He made himself comfortable on the edge of the bed and patted a section of the mattress.

She folded her hands across her middle. "You shot eleven under par for the weekend and that was nine strokes ahead of the number two man."

"I realize I played well, but there wasn't much pressure."

She cocked her head. "You've always been your worst enemy. You are the pressure."

He chuckled. "That's true. But also not the point. Without having someone as good as Tom on the leaderboard, I don't have a care in the world. Until I start consistently landing in the money week after week against the Toms of this world, it's not going to mean much to me."

"Don't let my father hear you say that."

"He agrees with me," Jack said. "He wants me to play in the Masters this year."

"That's in two months. Is he nuts?"

"We both must be, because I said I'd do it on one condition."

"Shit. You want me to caddy."

He nodded. "I want you to stick with me through my first major, and then I'll find someone else. I know this is going to be tough on you and on Bri, but I figure there are some trips we can take her on."

"You want her to travel with us?" Courtney splayed her hand across her middle and stared at him with wide eyes. "Wouldn't that be a major distraction?"

"Neither she nor you could ever be a negative in my life. All either of you do is bring a smile to my face."

"Oh boy." Courtney sat on the edge of the bed. "Who are you and what did you do with Jack?"

"What does that mean?"

"I've never heard you talk like that before. It's so sweet, kind, and weird."

He laughed. "But it's all true." He took her chin between his thumb and index finger. "I have a confession to make."

"Yeah. What's that?"

"I didn't come back here just to play golf. I came here because I'm in love with you."

She smacked his chest with the palm of her hand playfully, as if he were joking. "You what?"

"You heard me." He frowned. "I love you, Courtney. I think I was in love with you when you were seventeen, as inappropriate as that might have been."

She opened her mouth, but no words came out.

"You don't have to say it back, not yet anyway. I know it's a lot and its fast, even though it's always been there."

She bolted upright. "No. No. No." She paced at the foot of the bed, shaking her head.

"Are you telling me you don't feel the same way?" Perhaps he'd read the situation all wrong. Wouldn't be the first time.

"It doesn't matter how I feel. You and me in a long-term relationship isn't possible. Not with Tom lurking in the background. I can't—I won't—do that to Bri."

"And if I have a solution to that problem?"

She stopped pacing, dropped her hands to her sides, and gawked at him. "He's her father. Unless he dies, he's in her life. I can't change those facts. Having you in my life is a new challenge for me to navigate with Tom and that's fine, as long as we're friends. But if we take it to the next level—"

"We already have."

She let out an exasperated sigh. "I'm not talking about sex, and you know it. Tom will insert himself so deep into our lives, or he'll find a way to take Bri from me, and I won't have that. Not even for you." She took a couple of steps back, curling her fingers around the doorknob. "And yes, I love you, but I love my daughter more. No offense."

"None taken," he said, tapping his fingers against his chest in tune with his heartbeat.

She loved him.

That was a start.

Now all he had to do was find a way to get Tom out of their lives, and he figured Taylee had all the answers.

13

"What are we doing here, Jack?" A few days later Courtney sat at the picnic table at a park three towns over. Things had been awkward since they'd both said how they felt, but it wasn't horrible, and it hadn't affected his game.

That was a good thing.

"You'll find out soon enough." He sat across from her with a solemn expression, and that scared her.

"Why can't you just tell me?"

"Because this isn't my story to tell." He pointed toward the parking lot. "It's hers."

Courtney glanced over her shoulder and gasped.

Taylee had just handed a toddler over to a handsome man who kissed her gently on the lips before taking the little boy toward the swings.

"I don't understand."

Jack stood. "She'll explain it to you." He bent over

and kissed her temple. "I'm going to go for a walk. Text me when you're done."

She and Taylee had never been friends. Taylee was a few years older and never really gave Courtney the time of day, especially after she'd married Tom. Courtney had always suspected there was some history there, but she honestly hadn't cared. Tom had a history with most women.

"Hi, Courtney." Tentatively, Taylee sat down. She picked at the skin on the side of her thumb.

"I'm sorry, but I'm really confused. Jack hasn't told me anything."

"I know. I didn't want him to." A tear rolled down Taylee's cheek. "Until Jack called me the other day, the only other people who know the truth are my husband and my mother. Now Jack knows, and I'm going to tell you."

"The truth about what?"

"Tom," Taylee said flatly. "And what he did to me the night of the Langley party."

Courtney's heart dropped to her gut like a cement brick tossed into the ocean. "I'm so sorry about what happened that night."

Taylee nodded. "Thank you. This is going to sound weird considering what I just said, but I still don't remember, which might be a blessing. But I do know who raped me."

"If you don't remember, how can you know?"

Taylee swiped at her cheeks. She turned and waved

to the little boy she'd come with. "That's my son. His name is Oliver."

"Is that his father?" Courtney asked.

"In the true sense of the word, yes. But Steve and I have only been married for a year, and he came into our lives when Oliver was one. He just turned three a couple of months ago. He's the most amazing little boy in the world, and I can't imagine my life without him, but I never want his biological father to know about him."

"I wish Tom never knew about Bri. He's been making my life a living hell for years. I do my best to keep her out of the middle, but it's impossible sometimes." Courtney lifted her water bottle, bringing it to her lips. "Who is Oliver's father?"

"Do the math, Courtney."

Courtney spit out her water. In the back of her mind, she'd been forming the same thought, but her heart hadn't wanted to go there.

"Tom raped me that night, and I ended up pregnant with Oliver. I never told anyone I was pregnant until I was close to six months, and by then, Tom had been cleared of any suspicion. Deep down, I knew it had been him, but the only way to prove it would be a paternity test, and I saw what he was doing to you." Taylee paused to wipe the tears away again. "And your daughter and I couldn't have that for my child."

Courtney did her best to hold back her own tears. Taylee didn't need her pity. She needed her empathy and understanding. Courtney reached out and took her hand. "I think if the tables were turned, I would have done the same thing, but I hate to ask, how do you know Oliver is Tom's?"

"Because I did my own private paternity test." Taylee pulled out an envelope from her purse. "I had someone I know that was close to Tom get a sample of his hair. This is proof that Oliver is his child. I'm so sorry, Courtney, for everything that Tom has done to you and your daughter. I wish that I had faith back then that this would have been enough to prove that Tom was the one who raped me and that he'd have to pay for his crime. I want you to know that all I've been doing is protecting my son. I didn't keep this to myself for any other reason. I never wanted to hurt you or your daughter. But I don't want Tom to have a claim to Oliver."

"I don't blame you for that." Courtney held the envelope in her hands. "And I wouldn't want you to risk your son's happiness for anything." She pushed the envelope back. "There is no reason for you to tell the world that Tom is Oliver's father."

"I'm not doing it for that reason. When Jack called and told me a little bit of what you've been going through, I realized that I've enabled Tom to continue with his criminal ways. The world needs to know Tom is a rapist. I'm not the only one, you know."

Courtney nodded. She knew because while she'd been his wife, he'd done the same thing to her, and she'd done nothing about it.

"I'm tired of being afraid."

"Oh boy, do I know that feeling," Courtney said.

"I've spoken to a lawyer and the detective that was in charge of my case. While paternity alone doesn't prove he raped me, his statement about how he and I have never slept together will help us prove he did. That and I've talked to one other girl I know he raped. She's willing to come forward. I believe more will as well."

Tears flowed freely from Courtney's eyes. "I don't know what to say."

"There's nothing to say. We're in this together." Taylee moved to the other side of the table and hugged Courtney. "Together, we'll make sure Tom goes to jail where he belongs."

Courtney waved to Taylee and her family as they pulled out of the parking lot. She leaned against her car and waited for Jack to return. He'd texted that he was only a few minutes away.

That was five minutes ago.

She scanned the area and found him strolling in her direction carrying a couple of sodas and a bag from a food truck around the corner. She took the cold beverage and twisted the top, taking a long swig. "How did you know about Taylee and her son?"

"I saw her mom about a year ago. She filled me in on a few details, but not all of them. But over time, it started to click, and I decided to give Taylee a call.

When I told her about you and Bri, she filled me in on the rest."

"Wow." Courtney still struggled to process the information. "Part of me is pissed as hell at you."

"Why?" Jack took a blanket and spread it out on the grass. He sat down with the bag of food as if this were just any other normal conversation.

Which it was anything but.

But her stomach was screaming for sustenance, so she joined him, digging into the Caesar chicken wrap he'd brought while she continued to try to wrap her brain around what just happened.

"You went behind my back."

"I wasn't sure she had anything we could use to go after Tom," Jack said. "Or if she'd actually give it to us, much less want to go after him criminally. I didn't want to get your hopes up until we knew something for sure."

She couldn't be mad at him when he made such perfect sense. "Does my father know?"

Jack shook his head. "I figure we can tell him together at home this afternoon, although I did tell him that I thought I had some information that might help you get rid of Tom, and he told me to just do it."

"Well, I'm glad you did, but I don't want Taylee or her family to be dragged through the mud for me."

"She wouldn't be doing this if she wasn't ready," Jack said.

"What do we do next?"

"We don't do anything. Taylee will hand everything

over to the district attorney. They will take it from there."

"And what if Tom gets away with it?" Courtney asked, tears forming in her eyes. "What do we do then?"

"I don't think he will, but if the worst case happens, we stick together and deal with it." He took her hand and pressed it against his chest. "I love you, Courtney. I want to be with you and Bri always. I would do anything for you."

"Anything?" she asked with a coy smile.

"Yes. Anything."

"Will you come with me and Bri to Disney Orlando after the Masters?"

"Consider it a date." He leaned in and kissed her tenderly.

"I love you, Jack."

CHAPTER 14

SIX MONTHS LATER...

Jack sat in the back of the courtroom holding Courtney's hand. She squeezed so hard he thought she might actually break a bone.

Her father sat on the other side.

Taylee and her husband sat in the row in front of them.

Three other women who had come forward with allegations of rape also sat in the courtroom.

The trial had gone on for a week, and Tom still denied any wrongdoing, though he never took the stand in his own defense, but the evidence the district attorney had gathered had been quite damning.

Jack's only regret had been how this affected Bri. They had tried and tried to keep her from hearing about any of it, but she saw it on the television one night and had way too many adult questions. Both Courtney and her father struggled to answer them, but

Bri shocked them all when she told them she wanted a divorce from her biological father.

She even went as far as to ask the psychologist they had been sending her to if that was possible. And at the end of the day, Tom agreed to give up his parental rights, regardless of the outcome of the trial, and since the beginning of the ordeal, he hadn't tried to contact Bri at all.

That was both good and bad news. It was going to take some time and a lot of therapy for Bri to get through all this, but she would because she had a loving family and an extended support system to help guide her through it.

"Has the jury reached a verdict?" the judge asked.

"We have, Your Honor," the presiding juror said as he handed the security guard a piece of paper.

The judge opened it. "We the jury find the defendant guilty of rape in the first degree on all four counts."

A collective gasp filled the room.

Courtney leaned into Jack, squeezing his hand even harder.

"I want to thank the jury for their service," the judge said. "Sentencing will be tomorrow morning at nine. Bailiff, will you please take the defendant into custody." The judge hit his gavel. "This court is now adjourned."

Jack stood, taking Courtney into his arms.

She rested her head on his shoulder and cried. "It's finally over, isn't it?"

"It is," he said softly, stroking her hair. "So, does this mean we can get married now?"

She glanced up at him and smiled. "Yes. But I have one stipulation."

He arched a brow. "Do I want to know?"

"The first time I got married it was at town hall."

"Me too," he said with a chuckle.

"Well, this time, I want a big wedding. The white dress. The church. My father walking me down the aisle. Bri as the flower girl. Nicole as my maid of honor. The whole ball of wax."

"Babe, I wouldn't want to marry you any other way."

"There's one other little issue we need to discuss." She took his hand and raced out of the courtroom, dragging him down the hallway.

"Where are you taking me?"

She pulled him through the main doors, around the corner, and into the courtyard. "I didn't want to say this in front of everyone, only because I've only done the home test."

"Home what? Babe, you've lost me."

Her smile was as bright as the sun, and she giggled like a schoolgirl. "Do you think we can throw a church wedding together in a month?"

"I suppose we can, but we can't expect a ton of people to show up on such short notice."

"That's fine because I don't want to be fat when I marry you."

"Fat? Again, totally lost."

She cupped his cheeks. "I love you, Jack, and all our hopes and dreams are coming true."

Normally, Jack had no problem following anything Courtney had to say, but right now, in this moment, he hadn't a clue. "I love you right back. I want to get married, and the sooner the better because I'm tired of sneaking in and out of your room at night because of your father's rules and because of Bri. But we've waited this long, so it doesn't have to be in a month if we need longer to plan the wedding you want."

"Well, the wedding isn't as important as being married to you, but it will have to be quick because soon I will be showing."

"Showing wh…oh, shit. Are you pregnant?" His heart jumped to the back of his throat. In the last couple of months, they'd talked about all sorts of things, and having more children had been one of them, but in the future.

Well, the future was now.

"The home test says I am. I have an appointment with the doctor tomorrow to confirm, but I know my body. I'm about as sure as I can be."

The air in his lungs left his body. A wave of dizziness washed over him. "I think I need to sit down." He managed to make it to one of the benches. "A baby."

"Are you okay with this?"

He nodded, pulling the envelope from the inside pocket of his suit coat. "I hadn't expected to become a father times two in the same day."

"What are you talking about?" She sat next to him, taking the paper in her hands.

"Since Tom gave up all parental rights, I thought I'd ask to legally adopt Bri once we married. I spoke to her therapist, and she thinks it's a good idea, if done correctly, and this is the plan she laid out for us. But only if you want me to. I love you and Bri so much that sometimes it hurts." He patted his chest. "And now I've got another one to love."

She pressed her palm against his cheek. "Biology doesn't make someone a father, and I know for a fact that Bri would love to be able to call you daddy, and I want to be able to call you husband."

"Then let's do this, wife."

About Jen Talty

Welcome to my World! I'm a USA Today Bestseller of Romantic Suspense, Contemporary Romance, and Paranormal Romance.

I first started writing while carting my kids to one hockey rink after the other, averaging 170 games per year between 3 kids in 2 countries and 5 states. My first book, IN TWO WEEKS was originally published in 2007. In 2010 I helped form a publishing company (Cool Gus Publishing) with NY Times Bestselling

Author Bob Mayer where I ran the technical side of the business through 2016.

I'm currently enjoying the next phase of my life...the empty NESTER! My husband and I spend our winters in Jupiter, Florida and our summers in Rochester, NY. We have three amazing children who have all gone off to carve out their places in the world, while I continue to craft stories that I hope will make you readers feel good and put a smile on your face.

Sign up for my Newsletter (https://dl.bookfunnel.com/6atcf7g1be) where I often give away free books before publication.

Join my private Facebook group (https://www.facebook.com/groups/191706547909047/) where I post exclusive excerpts and discuss all things murder and love!

Never miss a new release. Follow me on Amazon:amazon.com/author/jentalty
And on Bookbub: bookbub.com/authors/jen-talty

ABOUT THE AUTHOR

Welcome to my World! I'm a USA Today Bestseller of Romantic Suspense, Contemporary Romance, and Paranormal Romance.

I first started writing while carting my kids to one hockey rink after the other, averaging 170 games per year between 3 kids in 2 countries and 5 states. My first book, IN TWO WEEKS was originally published in 2007. In 2010 I helped form a publishing company (Cool Gus Publishing) with NY Times Bestselling Author Bob Mayer where I ran the technical side of the business through 2016.

I'm currently enjoying the next phase of my life...the empty NESTER! My husband and I spend our winters in Jupiter, Florida and our summers in Rochester, NY. We have three amazing children who have all gone off to carve out their places in the world, while I continue to craft stories that I hope will make you readers feel good and put a smile on your face.

Sign up for my Newsletter (https://dl.bookfunnel.com/6atcf7g1be) where I often give away free books before publication.

Join my private Facebook group (https://www.facebook.com/

groups/191706547909047/) where I post exclusive excerpts and discuss all things murder and love!

Never miss a new release. Follow me on Amazon:amazon.com/author/jentalty

And on Bookbub: bookbub.com/authors/jen-talty

ALSO BY JEN TALTY

BRAND NEW SERIES!

The Monroes

COLOR ME YOURS

COLOR ME SMART

It's all in the Whiskey

JOHNNIE WALKER

GEORGIA MOON

JACK DANIELS

JIM BEAM

Search and Rescue

PROTECTING AINSLEY

PROTECTING CLOVER

NY State Trooper Series

IN TWO WEEKS

DARK WATER

DEADLY SECRETS

MURDER IN PARADISE BAY

TO PROTECT HIS OWN

DEADLY SEDUCTION

WHEN A STRANGER CALLS

NY State Trooper Novella

HIS DEADLY PAST

Brand New Novella for the First Responders series

A spin off from the NY State Troopers series

PLAYING WITH FIRE

PRIVATE CONVERSATION

The Men of Thief Lake

REKINDLED

DESTINY'S DREAM

Federal Investigators

JANE DOE'S RETURN

THE BUTTERFLY MURDERS

The Aegis Network

THE LIGHTHOUSE

HER LAST HOPE

THE LAST FLIGHT

THE RETURN HOME

THE MATRIARCH

The Collective Order

THE LOST SISTER

THE LOST SOLDIER

THE LOST SOUL

Coming soon!

THE LOST CONNECTION

Special Forces Operation Alpha

BURNING DESIRE

BURNING KISS

BURNING SKIES

BURNING LIES

BURNING HEART

BURNING BED

REMEMBER ME ALWAYS

The Brotherhood Protectors

Out of the Wild

ROUGH JUSTICE

ROUGH AROUND THE EDGES

ROUGH RIDE

ROUGH EDGE

ROUGH BEAUTY

The Brotherhood Protectors

The Saving Series

SAVING LOVE

A Family Affair

Nightshade

A Christmas Getaway

Taking A Risk

Tee Time

The Twilight Crossing Series

THE BLIND DATE

SPRING FLING

SUMMER'S GONE

WINTER WEDDING

Witches and Werewolves

LADY SASS

ALL THAT SASS

Coming soon!

NEON SASS

PAINTING SASS

Boxsets

LOVE CHRISTMAS, MOVIES

UNFORGETABLE PASSION

UNFORGETABLE CHARMERS

A NIGHT SHE'LL REMEMBER

SWEET AND SASSY IN THE SNOW

SWEET AND SASSY PRINCE CHARMING

PROTECT AND DESIRE

SWEET AND SASSY BABY LOVE

CHRISTMAS AT MISTLETOE LODGE

THE PLAYERS: OVERCOMING THE ODDS

CHRISTMAS SHORTS

CHRISTMAS DREAMS

All That Glitters

INVINCIBLE SECRETS

UNFORGETABLE SUSPENSE

Nov*ellas*

NIGHTSHADE

A CHRISTMAS GETAWAY

TAKING A RISK

WHISPERS